Friedrich Glauser was born in Vienna in 1896. Often referred to as the Swiss Simenon, he died aged forty-two, a few days before he was due to be married. Diagnosed a schizophrenic, addicted to morphine and opium, he spent much of his life in psychiatric wards, insane asylums and, when he was arrested for forging prescriptions, in prison. He also spent two years with the Foreign Legion in North Africa, after which he worked as a coal miner and a hospital orderly. His Sergeant Studer crime novels have ensured his place as a cult figure in Europe.

Germany's most prestigious crime fiction award is called the Glauser prize.

Other Bitter Lemon books featuring Sergeant Studer

Thumbprint
In Matto's Realm
Fever

THE CHINAMAN

Friedrich Glauser

Translated from the German
by Mike Mitchell

BITTER LEMON PRESS
LONDON

BITTER LEMON PRESS

First published in the United Kingdom in 2007 by
Bitter Lemon Press, 37 Arundel Gardens, London W11 2LW

www.bitterlemonpress.com

Originally published in German as *Der Chinese*
in the *National-Zeitung*, Basel in 1938

First published in book form in German as *Der Chinese*
by Morgarten Verlag AG Zurich in 1939

This edition has been translated with the financial assistance of
Pro Helvetia, the Arts Council of Switzerland

swiss arts council
prɔhelvetia

German-language edition © Diogenes Verlag AG Zurich, 1989
English translation © Mike Mitchell, 2007

A CIP record for this book is available from the British Library

ISBN 978–1–904738–21–3

Typeset by RefineCatch Limited, Broad Street, Bungay, Suffolk
Printed and bound by
Cox & Wyman Ltd, Reading, Berks

Contents

A dead man on a grave and two men arguing

Studer switched off the engine, dismounted from his motorbike and marvelled at the sudden silence all around. In the fog, yellow, greasy and matted like unwashed wool, walls appeared, the gleam of a red-tiled roof. Then the sun pierced the mist, striking a round sign and making it shine like gold. No, it wasn't gold but some other, much less precious, metal, a flat disc with two eyes, a nose and a mouth drawn on it and spiky hair sticking out round the edge. An inscription dangled below the sign: The Sun Inn. Well-worn stone steps led up to a door, in the frame of which stood a very old man. Studer had the feeling he recognized him, but the old man seemed unwilling to acknowledge the sergeant, for he turned away and disappeared inside the inn. A gust set the fog swirling, and once more inn, door and sign vanished.

Again the sun pierced the greyness. A low wall on the right-hand side of the street appeared, glass beads glistened on wreaths, gold lettering on gravestones shone, and box leaves gleamed like emeralds.

Three figures were standing round a grave: an officer of the rural gendarmerie in uniform, to his right a smooth-shaven, elegantly clad man, who looked young, and to his left an oldish man with an unkempt blond beard streaked with white. The bitter argument that was raging between two of them could be heard out in the street.

Studer shrugged his shoulders, pushed his bike

alongside the worn-down steps, lifted it up onto its stand and went into the cemetery, towards the grave where two of the living were arguing while a third stood watch in silence.

And Sergeant Studer of the Bern Cantonal Police sighed despondently several times as he walked. He didn't have an easy life, he thought.

That morning the deputy governor had phoned police headquarters from Roggwil. The body of a certain Farny, he said, had been found in the cemetery of the village of Pfründisberg. For the last nine months this Farny had been living in the Sun Inn, and it was Brönnimann, the landlord, who had found the body and informed the village policeman. Merz, the policeman, had reported that the cause of death was a shot to the heart.

"So far I have not been able to put an investigation in train, but it looks suspicious to me. The doctor maintains it's a case of suicide. I do not agree! To be on the safe side, I feel it is important to have an experienced detective present. The cemetery's opposite the inn . . ."

"I know that," Studer had broken in as an unpleasant shiver ran down his spine. A July night had come to mind on which a stranger had foretold this murder . . .

"Oh, you know that, do you? Who is that on the line?"

"Sergeant Studer. The chief superintendent's busy."

"Ah, Studer! Good. Excellent. Come at once! I'll be waiting for you at the cemetery."

Studer gave another sigh, shrugged his powerful shoulders, scratched his thin, pointed nose and cursed silently. It would be just the same as always, of course. He wasn't a celebrated criminologist, although in earlier years he had studied a lot. An intrigue had cost him his position as chief inspector with the Bern City Police;

2

he'd had to start from the bottom again with the cantonal force and had quickly risen to the rank of sergeant. Yet, although he'd been demoted, although he had enemies, he was always the one who was sent when there was a difficult case. This time too. After the telephone conversation Studer had reported to the superintendent and mentioned what had happened that July night. "Off you go, then, Studer. But don't come back until you're sure, until the case's solved. Right?"

"If I must . . . Cheerio." Studer had got on his bike and set off. The July night had been exactly four months ago, the night when he had met the stranger with the Swiss name of Farny. A stranger who was now dead . . .

"You can thank your lucky stars, yes, you can thank your lucky stars, Herr Deputy Governor, that I'm about to retire from my practice. Otherwise you'd have a few awkward questions to answer. You may well laugh! Putting the whole of the cantonal police on the alarm . . . er . . . on the alert for an obvious suicide, yes, a suicide!"

That was the oldish man with the profuse blond beard, streaked with white, round his wide mouth. The elegant, smooth-shaven gentleman raised his hands, clad in brown kid gloves, to ward off these accusations.

"Herr Doktor Buff, I must ask you to moderate your tone. After all, I am here in an official capacity . . ."

"Official capacity! Hahaha! Don't make me laugh." Why are the two of them speaking High German and not dialect? Studer thought. "You say you're an official? Any official could see at a glance that what we have here is a suicide, *a suicide*, Herr Deputy Governor."

"A murder, Herr Doktor Buff, yes, *a murder*. If you can't even distinguish between a murder and a suicide at your age . . ."

"At my age?! At my age?! A young mooncalf like you! Yes, a mooncalf, I stick by that word . . . trying to tell an old doctor like me what's a murder and what's not!"

"My instructions state that in cases of doubt an experienced detective must always . . ."

Studer had stopped listening. A little verse crept into his mind:

Things have happened on the Moon
That made the Mooncalf change his tune;
Honeymoon and Loondemyell
Both ran off with Mademoiselle . . .

But he called himself to order. It wasn't respectful to be thinking of amusing nonsense poems beside a dead body.

The body: the face of an old man, a white moustache, drooping down over the corners of his mouth, soft, like the skeins of silk women use for fine needlework. Narrow, slanting eyes . . . It was the man Studer had met during a night in July four months ago. From the very first moment he'd called him "the Chinaman".

While the old country doctor, looking shabby in his threadbare overcoat, continued to argue with the elegantly clad deputy governor, Studer recalled that night in July for the third time that morning. And if the memory of that remarkable experience had been vague the first two times, now it was clear, vivid, and he began to hear the words that had been spoken as well . . .

With a voice that sounded like the angel of peace as he interrupted the argument of the two fellow countrymen, he asked in his Bernese accent, "Who is it who's buried here?"

4

It was Dr Buff who replied. "The warden of the poorhouse lost his wife ten days ago."

"Hungerlott?"

The doctor nodded. His hair was rather long at the back and over his ears.

"Can you explain, Doctor Buff," the deputy governor said, "how a suicide can shoot himself in the heart, when the bullet has not made a hole in his coat or his jacket, not even in his shirt or waistcoat? Is that a suicide, Sergeant? You can see for yourself, the clothes are all buttoned up. That's the way we found the body. But he was shot through the heart."

Studer nodded, his thoughts elsewhere.

"And the gun?" Dr Buff squawked. "Isn't that the gun next to the dead man's hand? Isn't that suicide?"

Studer looked at the heavy gun, a Colt that he recognized. He nodded, nodded – and then said nothing more for five minutes because the night of 18 July was flickering through his mind like a film . . .

Memories

It was mere chance that Studer had stopped in Pfründisberg that evening. He'd forgotten to fill up in Olten, so he'd gone to the Sun Inn.

He went in. By the door in the side room was an iron stove, gleaming silver because it had been coated with aluminium paint. Four men were sitting round a table playing *Jass*. Studer shook himself like a big St Bernard, there was a lot of dust on his leather jacket. He sat down in one corner. No one took any notice. After a while he asked if you could get a can of petrol here. One of the card players, a little old man wearing a cardigan with linen sleeves sewn on, said to his partner in thick dialect, "'E wants a can o' petrol."

"Hmm . . . A can o' petrol . . ."

Silence. The room was hot and stuffy because the windows were closed. Through the glass you could see the green wood of the shutters. Studer was surprised no barmaid appeared to ask him what he wanted. The old man's partner said, "You forgot to count the king and queen."

Studer stood up and asked the way out onto the terrace. The room was too hot for him and, anyway, at the card table was a skinny man with a goatee whom Studer knew – the warden of the poorhouse in Pfründisberg, Hungerlott by name. An unpleasant man he'd got to know when he was a corporal in the cantonal police and had to escort people from the police station to Pfründisberg. That evening especially he didn't feel like chatting with Hungerlott.

"The corridor at the back," said the old man – he couldn't miss it.

When Studer stepped out into the open air he breathed more freely, despite the fact that it was close. Huge clouds were squatting on the horizon, a tiny moon, no bigger than an unripe lemon, was at its zenith casting its sparse light over the landscape. Then it disappeared and the only thing that was brightly lit in the area was the ground floor of a large building about four hundred yards from the inn. The sergeant leaned on the balustrade and looked out over the silent countryside; close in front of him was a maple, the leaves on the nearest branch were so clearly lit he could count each one. When he turned around to see where the light was coming from, he saw, through a window that gave onto the terrace, a lamp and a man writing. No curtains over the windows . . .

The man was sitting at a table with five exercise books covered in oilcloth piled up beside his right elbow; he was well on his way to filling the sixth book. How did a visitor come to be writing his memoirs in a little village like Pfründisberg?

Pfründisberg: a poorhouse, a horticultural college, two farms. The only thing that gave the hamlet any importance was the fact that the larger village of Gampligen, a mile and a half away, buried its dead in Pfründisberg.

All that went through Studer's mind as he stood at the window watching the solitary man tirelessly writing away in his exercise book. A white moustache hung down over the corners of his mouth, his cheekbones were prominent, and he had slant eyes. Before he had

7

exchanged a word with the stranger, Studer's name for him was "the Chinaman".

The sergeant would probably not have made the acquaintance of the man on that evening of 18 July had he not had a slight mishap. Was it the dust from the country lane? Was it the start of a cold? To put it briefly, Studer sneezed.

The stranger's reaction to this innocent sound was remarkable. He leaped up in such a hurry that he knocked his chair over, and his right hand went to the side pocket of his camelhair smoking jacket. With two rapid steps to the side he was by the window, seeking cover in the embrasure. With his left hand he grasped the handle of the window and flung it open. A brief silence. Then the man asked, "Who's there?"

Studer stood in the bright light, his massive figure casting a broad shadow on the balustrade.

"Me," he said.

"Don't be so stupid!" the stranger barked. "Will you tell me who you are?"

The man spoke German with an English accent. English? The odd thing was that there was something Swiss peeking out from beneath this foreign accent, something Studer couldn't quite put his finger on. Perhaps it was the stress he put on the word "will", which came out as "*wiu*".

"Bern Cantonal Police," the sergeant said good-humouredly.

"Identification."

Studer showed it, though with a heavy heart; the photograph on his identity card always irked him. He felt it made him look like a lovesick sea lion.

The stranger handed it back, but that did not resolve the situation, for the sergeant knew the man had a revolver in his jacket pocket. The thought of being shot in the stomach was decidedly unpleasant. The word "laparotomy" buzzed around inside his head like an irritating mosquito, and he breathed a sigh of relief when the stranger finally took his right hand out of his pocket.

Now Studer asked, quietly, with excessive politeness and in his best High German, "And now might *I* ask to see *your* papers?"

"*Surely*," the man said in English, then reverted to German. "Certainly."

He went over to the table, opened a drawer and came back with a passport.

A Swiss passport! Issued in the name of James Farny, place of origin: Gampligen, Bern Canton, born 13 March 1878, issued in Toronto, Canada, renewed 1903 in Shanghai, renewed in Sydney, renewed in Tokyo, renewed . . . renewed . . . renewed in 1928 in Chicago USA . . . crossed into Switzerland 18 February 1931 in Geneva . . .

"So you've been back in Switzerland for five months, Herr Farny?" Studer asked.

"Five months, yes. Wanted to see my home country, the *Heimat*, once more." There it was again, that sound. The Chinaman said "He-imat", separating the "e" and "i", while an Englishman would surely have made it a long "ai". "Are you a . . .?" He was clearly struggling with his German. "A . . . senior police officer? A . . . what do you call them, an . . . inspector and not just a plain *constable*?" The last word was in English again.

"Sergeant," said Studer good-humouredly.

"Then you would be called in when there's a murder, for example?"

Studer nodded.

"You see, it is possible that I will be murdered," said the Chinaman. "Perhaps today, perhaps tomorrow, perhaps in a month's time. It might perhaps take even longer. You'll have a drink?"

The storm

Silence ... Now the clouds were not squatting on the horizon any more. They had risen up, covering the sky. A flash of lightning slashed the dark in two, the violent clap of thunder that followed set off a crackling and rumbling that died away beyond the hills. It had obviously caused a short circuit. The lamp in the Chinaman's room went out, but Herr Farny was clearly prepared for such emergencies. Hardly five seconds had passed before the light from a torch was playing over the balcony. And Studer observed that the well-travelled guest was holding the torch in his left hand, while his right hand gripped the butt of what was almost a miniature machine gun. Another flash of lightning, and then, like an axe hitting a beech-wood block, the drops of rain fell on the maple leaves. He could count them: five, six, seven – silence again – then finally the murmur of rain. The smell of wet dust and damp wood rose up to the balcony; the flowers gave off their scent.

The light flared up again. Farny put his gun away in the table drawer, rinsed out his glass, which was on the washstand, and filled it with a pungent yellow liquid. There was a picture of a white horse on the label.

"Have a drink," he said. "It's a good whisky. You can trust it." Studer tossed back half the glass and then broke out coughing, which made Farny laugh. "Strong, isn't it? Not used to it? But it's still better than your rotgut, what d'you call it? *Bätziwasser*?" He took the glass, still half full, out of Studer's hand, drank it and said, using the familiar "*Du*": "There, Jakob! We're whisky brothers. That's almost as good as blood brothers. You'll avenge me if I'm murdered."

The sergeant thought this Herr Farny was a bit off his rocker, and being addressed by his first name irritated him too. How would he look, he, a sergeant in the Bern Cantonal Criminal Investigation Department, if this James Farny should turn out to be a con man? Then he'd have to arrest him, and the first thing he would do would be to inform the examining magistrate that he was on first-name terms with the policeman who'd nabbed him. So when the stranger filled the tumbler with whisky again and offered it to him, the sergeant said a polite no thank you.

The Chinaman wasn't bothered by this refusal. He said impassively, "So you don't want a drink, Brother Jakob? Then I'll drink by myself." He emptied the glass. "But," he went on, "I'm going to introduce you to all the people who could be my murderer."

For a moment Studer thought of phoning the psychiatric clinic in Waldau; this Herr Farny was obviously suffering from paranoia. But then he dismissed the thought and agreed to go with him. The latter did not leave by the obvious route of the door but vaulted out of the window onto the balcony, grasped Studer by the arm and pulled him along with him. The sergeant was surprised to observe how agitated his companion was; he could clearly feel his fingers trembling. They were drumming softly on the leather of his jacket.

A fracas

James Farny led the sergeant to another room that was fairly full. The room with the gleaming silver aluminium stove must have been the landlord's private parlour. In the bar the two had just entered there were four old men in greasy blue overalls sitting by the door round a table on which was a half-pint bottle filled with a light-yellow liquid. By the window were five more, dressed in similar dirty blue overalls, and these men, too, had low, thick-sided tumblers in front of them.

"*Bätziwasser*," said Herr Farny contemptuously.

Sitting at a round table in the middle of the room were four young lads in city suits with incredibly loud ties, their collars all askew. There was one among them who struck Studer right from the beginning. He looked older than the rest. He had a thin face with a pointed nose sticking out that was so long it looked like a caricature. The four young men were drinking beer. The barmaid was sitting behind the bar knitting. Her two fat brown plaits were pinned round her head like a bizarre wreath. Herr Farny made his way to the table next to the one where the young lads were sitting. There was an old farmer sitting at it, quietly enjoying a glass of wine.

"Well then, Schranz, how're things?" the Chinaman asked.

"Hmm," the old man mumbled.

"What's Brönnimann doing?"

"Playing *Jass* . . ." Herr Farny sat down, and Studer

did so too. There was definitely an unpleasant atmosphere in the room. There was tension, although it was impossible to say what was the cause. The four in blue by the door and the five in dirty overalls by the window looked at the two new arrivals, contempt smeared all over their faces.

It wasn't the storm that was causing the tension, nor Herr Farny's elegant clothes. Studer clearly heard the words "bloody cops" but couldn't tell which table it came from.

But how had the people found out there was a policeman among them? Of course! The police badge on his machine. But . . . why were the people from the poorhouse afraid of the police? And the lads in their city suits and crooked collars, who must surely be from the horticultural college?

"Brandy," Herr Farny called out. "Huldi, two brandies. And make sure it's the good stuff." Shyly the barmaid came over. Her complexion was striking. It looked as if her skin were covered in mildew. "Certainly, Herr Farny," she said and, "With pleasure, Herr Farny."

But she never got around to bringing the order. All at once the four at the table by the door started bawling out "We don't want any cops in Pfründisberg" to the tune of "We don't want any Krauts in Switzerland". They stood up. One picked up the bottle, the others armed themselves with the thick-sided tumblers, and they advanced from two sides on the sergeant's table, still singing their stupid song.

The Chinaman balanced on the back legs of his chair, his red leather slippers dangling from his toes. He seemed to be enjoying the whole business.

"Afraid, Inspector?" he asked, stroking the white, silken strands of hair covering the corner of his mouth.

Studer shrugged his massive shoulders. But when

14

the lads from the horticultural school decided to take part in the rumpus, and the one with the caricature of a nose grasped a beer bottle to join the men from the poorhouse, James Farny said, in a voice of command, as if he were talking to a dog, "Down, Äbi."

The young man sat down again. Studer had stayed sitting in his chair, legs wide, elbows on his thighs, hands clasped, hunched forward. And, in fact, there was nothing to fear, since the door to the neighbouring room suddenly opened, and the four card-players came in.

It was strange how they appeared, one after the other, framed in the doorway. Each one looked like a separate picture.

Warden Hungerlott was the first and hesitated before crossing the threshold. The goatee on his chin made his face look pointed.

"What's all this noise? Drinking schnapps again? Didn't I forbid it?"

The old men in their greasy overalls retreated towards the door. Now Hungerlott was in the light from the lamp.

"Ah, Sergeant Studer. How are you, how are you?"

Studer muttered something incomprehensible.

A second figure, massive, his sleeves rolled up to reveal the blond hair on his arms, appeared in the doorway and immediately started to berate the lads. "How often have I told you not to come to the inn in the evening? Can't you do what you're told? Off you go now, quick march!"

That must be the principal of the horticultural college. A triple chin oozed down over his raw-silk shirt, a white-gold chain dangled over the curve of his paunch, the wedding ring on his right hand cut deeply into the flesh of his finger.

His students disappeared.

Only now did the little old man appear, bowed down and panting. He croaked, "What's been going on, Huldi? Couldn't you have called me?" A fit of coughing put a stop to his questions.

Following close behind was his *Jass* partner, Gerber, the farmer, who was such a nondescript little man no one paid him any attention.

All that was left of the men from the poorhouse in the almost empty room was the smell of *Bätziwasser* and cheap tobacco. Now even that disappeared when the barmaid obeyed the college principal's command to open the window. Air cleaned by the thunderstorm poured into the room.

And then the miracle happened. All at once there were six crystal glasses on the table in the middle (crystal in a village inn!). Herr Farny poured the drinks and, with a wink to the sergeant, introduced those present: "Herr Hungerlott, warden of the poorhouse, you already know, Sergeant, but here, may I introduce Herr Ernst Sack-Amherd, principal of Pfründisberg Horticultural College. Then Herr Alfred Schranz, farmer; Herr Albert Gerber, farmer; the barmaid, Hulda Nüesch; and, finally, Rudolf Brönnimann, the esteemed landlord of the Sun Inn ... – And this is Inspector Jakob Studer. Gentleman, raise your glasses."

Studer recalled that at the time it had struck him this Herr Farny must have a remarkable memory. He had only glanced briefly at the sergeant's identification but had not only remembered his surname but his Christian name as well. He did seem to have forgotten they were "whisky brothers", since he had stopped addressing his guest by the informal "*Du*".

"It's heartbreaking," said Hungerlott, "but you cannot get the men to give up schnapps. I beg you not

16

to tell the people in Bern what you've seen here, Sergeant. When all's said and done, they work the whole week, and on Saturday they each get a franc and a packet of tobacco. It has to do them for the following week. What do they do to forget their wretched state? Brandy's too dear for them, so they drink *Bätziwasser*. Pauperism, Sergeant, is the blight of our society. Do I have to explain the word 'pauperism'?"

Studer stared at the table. He had put on a non-committal expression and wore it like a mask. He raised his eyes; there was a blank look in them.

"*Pauper*," the Warden began his lecture, "means 'poor' in Latin. Pauperism deals with the problem of poverty. Here in Switzerland, of course, we have to consider the whole question of the welfare system as well, which is just as complicated as . . ."

He was interrupted by Gerber. "But you didn't note down the points for the king and queen in the last game." Brönnimann retorted that it was a damned lie: of course he'd noted them down. And Studer said he'd asked for a can of petrol ages ago, might it be possible finally to get one?

"Exactly! The man asked for some petrol." Gerber supported the sergeant's request.

For a moment there was silence. Then Herr Sack-Amherd, the principal of the horticultural college, said that, yes, it wasn't always that easy with the student nurserymen, most of the lads had already been self-employed and had no sense of discipline.

"And what can *I* say?" That was Hungerlott joining in again. "They allocate to me everybody they can't send to Witzwil Labour Camp, to Thorberg Prison or St Johansen Clinic. There are some among them who've done ten years, and I'm supposed to keep them occupied. You should see the complaints, Sergeant! 'We have to work for nothing; our work keeps the fine gentlemen in luxury.' And that when, to be perfectly honest with you, we don't even cover our costs. Each year the state has to stump up at least – at least, I say! – twenty thousand francs, or our accounts would be in a pretty mess. I'm starting to feel like a travelling sales-man, I've even bought a car and have to make the rounds of our customers. The competition from the other state institutions! That's the problem! The luna-tic asylums, the prisons, they're all supplying goods produced on the premises. The result is, we get the crazy situation where one institution is trying to steal the others' custom . . ."

"It was a can o' petrol he wanted," Gerber interrupted.

"I'm going, I'm going," the landlord snarled and stomped out of the room.

The rest clinked glasses, drank and stayed silent. Then Herr Sack-Amherd too started to moan bitterly about the government. In the old days the peasants revolted because they were required to pay tithes. And nowadays? Nowadays not a soul objected when they had to shell out twelve or even fourteen per cent income tax. And that, in his modest opinion, was more than a tithe. But who dared to complain about these infringements, these financial infringements? No one! And why . . .?

Brönnimann appeared in the door. He'd managed to find a can of petrol, would the Sergeant come and have a look but hurry up about it . . .?

Herr Farny stood up along with Studer. He'd see his guest out, he said. There was a general farewell. The handshake of Hungerlott, the poorhouse warden, was very sticky. It was as if he couldn't free his fingers from Studer's hand. Herr Sack-Amherd's farewell was noticeably briefer, and the two farmers, Gerber and Schranz, simply muttered something incomprehensible. Then Studer was at the bottom of the worn steps. Brönnimann, the landlord, disappeared into a shed in order, as he said, to fetch some petrol. The Chinaman was the only one left with the sergeant.

"Now you've seen everyone, Inspector," said Herr Farny. "*Almost* everyone. From what I heard today, there's another young lad in the house whom I couldn't introduce to you. He's afraid of the police, if you understand what I mean. Otherwise . . . As I said, almost everyone was present."

Herr Farny was silent for a while, then he jerked up his head and looked the sergeant in the eye. The lamp over the door to the inn – with, dangling above it, the sign with the spiky hair sticking out that was supposed to represent the sun – shone on their faces from above, casting dark shadows on them. The Chinaman placed his light, old-man's hand on the sergeant's powerful shoulder and said:

"So you'll avenge me."

Say nothing! Farny did not lower his eyes. "Avenge me," he repeated. "You'll think this is childish, Inspector. Perhaps you're right. But I don't want *him* to triumph."

"Him?" the sergeant asked. "Which him?"

At that the Chinaman smiled. It was not a Bernese smile at all, almost non-European. "Who? If I only knew. I don't know, that is something *you* will have to find out. But I have confidence in you. I can see what kind of person you are, Inspector, without having to see a sample of your handwriting, without knowing your date of birth. You, Inspector, are like a diesel engine running on heavy-duty fuel oil. It takes a long time for you to work up to full speed, but once you're running, you take every obstacle like a tractor, like a tank. I know, you've been thinking this Farny's mad, he's suffering from paranoia. You'll see that Farny was right. Tomorrow? The day after? In a month? In two? Three? Eventually you'll see he was right, and then you'll have some work to do. Good night, Inspector, sleep well. I hope you have a pleasant journey home."

No handshake, no noise. James Farny, the Chinaman, had disappeared without a sound. Up the steps? Round the corner of the building?

Coughing and panting and spitting, the landlord came out of the shed with a gallon can of petrol. Studer filled his tank, paid, kicked the starter and drove off into the silent night. There were still lights on in a few of the houses in the hamlet of Pfründisberg; he left them behind him. The summer night was fresh.

All that had happened on 18 July.

And today was 18 November.

Three months was the maximum delay Farny had reckoned before his murder. He had been one month out. Four months had passed since 18 July.

Three locales

Studer's silence beside the body of the Chinaman, as he still called Herr Farny in his own mind, had presumably been so short that it did not strike the others. The recall of that July night had probably lasted only a few seconds. The events had run quickly through his mind, without the others being aware of what was going on there. And the sergeant did not want to tell either the old village doctor of Gampligen, with his profuse white hair tumbling over his ears and coat collar, or the elegant deputy governor, whose waspwaisted coat was very stylish but surely not very warm, about that night in July. So he asked an apparently naïve question.

"What's the dead man called and where did he live?"

The deputy governor cleared his throat. "A stranger," he said, "although he came from Gampligen. He ran away from home when he was thirteen and was taken on as a cabin boy. Later he did all sorts of things, but as far as I've been able to ascertain, most of his activities were in China. Originally his first name was Jakob ..." That gave Studer a slight shock. "But he anglicized it and called himself James. He had a room in The Sun, though no one knew why he'd settled there. Was it the call of home, of Gampligen? Was he looking for relations? I suspect he has taken the answers to those questions to the grave with him."

"What did I tell you, Sergeant? Won't our deputy governor make an excellent member of the National

Council? He can talk, talk, talk. Also, and this is the main point, he enjoys listening to his own prattle."

"Doctor Buff, I would beg you . . ."

"Beg away, beg away."

"I refuse to respond to any more of these insinuations. I have done my duty and brought in a man experienced in criminal investigation. The rest is none of my business."

"You're washing your hands of the affair, Deputy Governor. Of course – Pontius Pilate was a governor too."

"Gentlemen . . . gentlemen." Studer raised his hands, in their woollen gloves, to calm down both sides. "If you would allow me to point out one of the remarkable aspects of this case . . ."

"Point away, heehee, point away," croaked Dr Buff.

". . . then it would be" – Studer ignored the interruption – "the following. This case appears to be set in three locales: a village inn, a poorhouse and a horticultural college. The poorhouse seems to have the greatest involvement. Why was the body of the murdered man found on the grave of the late wife of the poorhouse warden, Herr Hungerlott?"

"You see, that just strengthens my theory of suicide," said Dr Buff with an air of wisdom as he scratched his forehead. "Love! You know what a devastating effect love can have on the human heart, Sergeant. The warden's wife was a beautiful woman. Perhaps – I say perhaps – this outsider fell in love with her. Perhaps her death was too much for him, and he killed himself . . ." The doctor's face was a tangle of wrinkles.

"Did you hear that, Sergeant? For an hour I've tried everything I can to persuade this doctor we're dealing with a murder, and what's his latest revelation? Suicide caused by unrequited love!"

Studer stopped listening to the quarrelsome pair. He bent over the body and started to go through the contents of the pockets. While he was doing so, he could not resist talking in his mind to the dead man. "You got on my nerves because you kept insisting on us being 'whisky brothers'. Forgive me, I didn't take you seriously, thought you were putting on an act or took yourself too seriously. Why didn't you tell me everything? Why didn't you ask me to stay with you? Perhaps I could have protected you. I have to admit I thought you'd read too many adventure stories. I thought you might have had some kind of "Revenge is Sweet" going through your mind. And now someone's shot you. What that doctor's saying's a load of rubbish. That natty deputy governor's right – just as you were right . . ."

The pockets were empty, so Studer turned to the official present, who was wearing grey spats. "Did you look through his pockets?"

"No, I just had a look at the wound."

"Me too," croaked Dr Buff. "But there was something else I observed. A shot has been fired from the gun beside his right hand."

Studer stood up and asked, "How do you know that, Doctor?"

"You only need to have a sniff at the muzzle, Sergeant."

To himself Studer said, "I'd rather send for an ambulance from Bern and get the body taken to the mortuary there than have you do the autopsy." What he said out loud was, "I'll keep you informed, Deputy Governor. Goodbye, Herr Doktor." Tapping the brim of his hat with two fingers, he left the graveyard. When he stopped at the gate and looked around he saw the two were once more arguing vehemently, while the village policeman was standing at the head of the grave, still as a statue. The three of them hid the body of the Chinaman, which lay on the freshly dug grave. The mist was thinning, sunlight poured through, making it shine like raw silk . . .

Fear

This time Studer went to the right room. He walked past the door to the landlord's private quarters and saw the stove coated with aluminium paint only in memory. Then he was in the bar. He heard a glass fall to the floor and smash. The barmaid, Hulda Nüesch, her plaits like a wreath round her head, was bending down behind the bar. It seemed to Studer that her complexion was even paler than on that long-ago July night.

"What's up, Huldi?" No reply.

He told her to bring him a large glass of red wine and some ham.

"Yes, Herr . . . Herr . . . Sergeant." Fearfully, the girl slipped out of the door.

In the bar it smelled of cold cigar smoke, of stale beer too. Studer went through the ceremony of lighting a Brissago, took a notebook out of his pocket and licked the end of his pencil.

Farny, James Jakob, he wrote, *born 13 March 1878, place of origin Gampligen.*

He had only seen these details once, briefly, but he remembered them as if the page from the passport that contained them was photographed on his mind. He continued to write in his tiny script:

Any relations?

Brothers? Sisters? Nieces?

Why was the body on Frau Hungerlott's grave?

Must have been shot while wearing his pyjamas. Find the pyjamas!

Phone Forensic . . .

He looked around the room. Behind the bar was a sideboard, the upper part of which was full of bottles. There was a telephone on the corner of the marble top. Studer pushed past the barmaid, who was washing glasses, dialled the number of the Institute for Forensic Medicine and asked to speak to Dr Malapelle. He told him what he wanted, half in Italian and half in German: the body of the man who had been shot was to be collected as soon as possible, an autopsy was necessary, he hoped he'd be able to come to Bern the next day to get the results. *Auf Wiedersehen . . .*

His Brissago had gone out, of course. While he was relighting it, he looked out of the window. Five hundred yards further on the plateau fell away steeply. On the other side of the valley the hazy glow of colourful autumn foliage, bordered by the dark green of pines, shone through the mist.

"There you are . . . there you are . . . Sergeant."

"*Meerci.*"

Studer filled his glass; it was the pink *ordinaire* of the region. The barmaid hurried out of the room, and the old man appeared.

"Ah! . . . Sergeant Studer . . . How's the snack?"

"Mhm." Studer chewed and observed Brönnimann from beneath his lowered lids. "It was you," he said, "who found the body?"

"Me? . . . Yes . . . as it happened."

"What were you doing out in the graveyard in the morning? Eh? It was still dark, wasn't it?"

"Takin' a little . . . Just goin' out for few minutes. Fresh air's good for you when you're my age . . ."

"And then you saw your guest? Dead?"

"Dead and done for, yes, Sergeant. But I didn't touch him!"

"Who said anything about touching? But sit down, sit down. You're going round and round the room like a . . ."

"Sorry. *Pardon.* If that's all right."

The old man called out, "Huldi! Bring another glass."

He couldn't leave the girl in peace. Once she'd brought the glass, she had to look sharp and bring a half carafe of wine. The innkeeper clinked glasses with the sergeant and wished him "Your good health", but his whole behaviour seemed put on. Brönnimann never looked the sergeant in the eye; he kept his gaze on the floor. The old man breathed heavily, panting and wheezing all the time, and when he talked, he kept being interrupted by fits of coughing.

"Yes, Sergeant, if you'd only listen to me. But an old man like me, what's 'e got to say that's worth hearin'? – *kherfkherfkherf.* Yerss. He was a nice man to have staying here, was Herr Farny, never any noise, never any fuss – quiet as a little mouse. Yerss. – *kherfkherfkherf* – And still 'e's been murdered." Coughing. Then the innkeeper went on: "If he could only tell what he knew! But like people said, better safe than sorry – *kherfkher-fkherf.* Important people came to this inn, the warden of the poorhouse, the principal of the horticultural college, members of the canton parliament, of the government – when they were inspecting the college and the poorhouse, of course – *kherfkherfkherf* – And you didn't want to get on the wrong side of important people . . .

"Do you know any of the dead man's relatives?" Studer asked. He'd skewered a piece of ham on his fork and was examining it critically.

"Relatives? Yerss, I could tell you a lot about 'is relatives. But you know, Sergeant, you have to be careful, you can easily open your mouth a bit too wide . . . If I were to tell you all the things that were said when that Anna died . . ."

"Anna Hungerlott? The warden's wife? What was her maiden name?"

"Er, Äbi . . ."

"Äbi?" Studer popped the piece of ham in his mouth and thought. Äbi? He'd heard that name before. But where? The July night came back to mind and two words the late James Farny had said. "Down, Äbi," he'd said to one of the students from the horticultural college.

"Was Anna related to someone from Pfründisberg?"

Brönnimann nodded and nodded. Her brother had gradated from the horticultural college. Studer smiled. Ah yes, those difficult words. But in the end of the day it didn't matter. Gradated or graduated, there wasn't much of a difference, the important thing was to be understood.

"Listen, Brönnimann, you didn't hear anything last night, did you?"

Silence. Then a little cry – the sound came from the direction of the bar. The old man turned around and barked at the barmaid, "Get on with yer work, Missie." Then he turned back to his guest, and his eyes were as blue as the flame of a spirit stove.

"The staff nowadays, Sergeant," he said. "It's enough to drive a man to despair."

"I asked you whether you heard a shot."

"A shot?" the old man repeated. There had been something, he thought, around half past two. He had heard a bang, but then a motorbike had driven past, and the bang could have come from the bike . . . the engine backfiring, something like that . . .

"But there was a shot, Brönnimann."

28

"You keep your nose out of other people's business, Missie," the old man told her sharply, but Studer was already licking the point of his pencil and making a new entry in his notebook.

"At half past two then, was it?" the sergeant asked. "Who was here yesterday evening?"

"Oh . . . *kherfkherfkherf* . . . Herr Hungerlott, the warden, Herr Sack-Amherd, the principal of the college, Gerber . . . we were playing *Jass*. And then two or three of the students . . ." The old man stopped.

"No one else?" Studer wanted to know. Again the answer came from behind the bar.

"There were two others. Why don't you want to name them, Brönnimann?"

"You hold yer tongue, Missie. Too much talk can be bad for you."

Studer resolved to get the girl to talk at the first opportunity. For the moment he concentrated on another question:

"Tell me, Brönnimann . . . why are you afraid?"

"Me, Sergeant? Me, afraid?"

"Yes, you," said Studer baldly, using the familiar, almost insulting "*Du*", at the same time thrusting his index finger at the old man's hollow chest. How different people were! You had to address some formally, be friendly to others – and then there were those who would only tell you what they knew when you were downright rude to them.

He wasn't afraid, the innkeeper protested, the very idea was ridiculous. Afraid! Then the old man got up, toddled over to the door, flung it open and slammed it shut behind him.

Studer's rudeness had had its effect. He stood up.

"Come on, Huldi," he said, "Show me the dead man's room."

"But you're not going to arrest him, are you, Sergeant?"

Aha! So there was someone in the inn who had a guilty conscience. Not the landlord, although the barmaid would probably have been delighted to get him locked up, no, someone else . . . Who? Could it be the one the Chinaman had spoken about during that evening in July? "From what I heard today there's another young lad in the house whom I couldn't introduce to you." Strange how well he could remember that sentence . . . Studer pretended to misunderstand what the girl had said.

"No, no, Huldi, I don't arrest dead men."

"Oh, you know who I mean, Sergeant."

"Me? I know nothing, nothing at all."

Huldi Nüesch, who wore her brown plaits pinned round her head like a wreath, led the way, Studer following. They went along a corridor with red tiles on the floor – they had white sand sprinkled over them. The barmaid opened a door on the left, and the two of them went into the late James Farny's room.

"Keep your fingers off our *rösti*!"

Huldi apologized to the sergeant. With all the fuss, she hadn't got round to tidying up.

Studer stood in the middle of the room, stuck his hands deep in the pockets of his coat, looked around and said he was glad nothing had been touched. The bed looked as if there had been a fight in it. The sheets and blankets were on the floor. The windows were closed. In the middle of the floor was a suitcase with labels of hotels from all over the world stuck on it. It was empty.

There was nothing on the table. Studer searched the wardrobe, the bedside table, under the mattress – the exercise books he remembered so well had disappeared.

Why had they been stolen? What did they say that was so important?

"Huldi," the sergeant said gently, "you remember the exercise books Farny used to write in? Did you ever happen to read one? Do you know what was in them?"

The girl nodded, kept on nodding. Then she said, like someone reciting a lesson they'd learned by heart: "After we left Hong Kong in 1912 we were caught in a typhoon. We had loaded rice for Bangkok and coolies for Sumatra. I ordered the first mate to lock the coolies in a room below deck . . ."

"That'll do fine," said Studer. "You don't remember anything else?"

"He never left the last one he was writing in lying

around open, he always locked it away in his suitcase. I did once get the chance to have a quick look at it. The bit I saw said, 'If God wants to punish a man, He sends him relatives.' "

"Were those the precise words?" Studer asked. The barmaid nodded.

And while she was nodding, a windowpane shattered.

"What on earth's that?" Studer asked. Huldi went to the window, flung it open and looked out into the misty afternoon air. She could see nothing, she said. Furious, the sergeant grabbed her by the arm and pulled her back. Someone had fired a shot into the room, he told her angrily and pushed her onto a chair. She sat there, her elbows on the table, her face buried in her hands.

"A shot?" she asked. "A shot!"

"Yes, a shot," Studer told her impatiently. He was striding up and down the room, his eyes fixed on the floor, looking – but he could see nothing. He bent down and found a lead ball under the bed. He picked it up. It was round, like a globe, but instead of the equator, someone had cut a groove into the lead and wedged a strip of paper in it. The sergeant carefully pulled it out and read the words that were typed on it:

Keep your fingers off our *rösti*!

Studer frowned, shook his head and muttered one word: "*Chabis!*"

But "a load of rubbish" did not seem to be the sergeant's only response to the incident. He kept the strip of paper in his hand, growling several times, "Keep your fingers off our *rösti*!"

It was obvious that the lead ball had not been shot

into the room with a rifle or even an airgun. Too much spoke against it.

Above all, the strip of paper wedged into the "equator" would have made it impossible to fire the ball. What kind of weapon could have been used?

The only possibility was a catapult, the kind of thing he'd used to shoot sparrows when he was a lad. A forked piece of wood or metal with lengths of rubber, square in cross-section, attached to each of the ends and joined together by a piece of leather. You put the ball-bearing, the stone – in brief, the missile – into the leather, which you held fast with the finger and thumb of your right hand, while you held the stem of the catapult in your left. Pull back the rubber, aim through the opening between the two prongs, let go, and the missile flies off and hits the sparrow or the window. Today it had been a windowpane, and the missile contained a typed warning.

Who felt called upon to send Sergeant Studer a warning? In the first place: was it meant seriously? Probably not, otherwise the "marksman" would presumably not have used a dialect word like *rösti*. You'd scarcely write, "Keep your fingers off our fried potatoes" to someone you intended to shoot. On the other hand, perhaps the form was intended to lull the recipient into a false sense of security . . .? Note to self: better keep a good lookout.

A stowaway

The mist was probably the reason why twilight fell so swiftly over the countryside. Studer switched the light on and drew the curtains. The barmaid was still sitting at the empty table, her chin resting in the hollow of her hands. When the sergeant looked more closely, he saw that large tears were running down her cheeks. And something she'd said came back to mind, something that was more like a question: "But you're not going to arrest him, are you, Sergeant?"

James Farny's room was well furnished, which meant there were at least two chairs. Since Huldi was sitting in one, he grasped the other, pulled it over to him, sat down astride it, leaned his arms on the backrest and his chin on his clasped hands.

"What's wrong, my girl?" he asked.

The silent tears turned into loud sobs.

"Lu . . . Ludwig, Sergeant."

"What's the matter with Ludwig? Where is he?"

"In my . . . my room."

"The things you've been getting up to," said Studer. "Wait here, I'll go and fetch Ludwig."

He left the room, fairly surprised not to catch the innkeeper listening at the door. He went up to the first floor – empty bedrooms – then up to the attic. Huldi's room was not difficult to find. There was dust on the floor outside the other doors, but at one it reflected the reddish light of the lamp. Studer knocked. No answer. He pressed down the handle and opened the door.

To the left of the window was a bed, with a blanket over the springs. To the right was a mattress on the floor. A young man, lying back with his head resting on his clasped hands, leaped up and stared at the sergeant. His hair was as yellow as straw, and his eyes such a dark blue they didn't remind you of a spirit flame, more of a mountain lake ... His cheap linen-mixture suit was crumpled ... and he definitely hadn't shaved for three days.

Studer gave a nod of satisfaction. The arrangement of the room clearly showed nothing unseemly had taken place. People were always shooting their mouths off about the immorality of modern youth – and here? Here a barmaid had slept on the springs to let her friend have the mattress. Studer's moustache quivered as a faint smile crossed his lips. They had even shared out the sheets – one for the girl, one for the lad – and the blankets too ... The girl would have spent the night shivering under her eiderdown and the lad under the blanket and his shabby coat.

"What's your name?"

"Ludwig Farny."

"Are you related to the dead man?"

"The dead man?"

"Yes. Don't you know that the Chin ... I mean that James Farny is dead?"

"Uncle Jakob?"

Studer pulled a face. Why did the Chinaman have to have the same first name as a detective sergeant from Bern?

"Yes, your Uncle Jakob."

"Dead? Uncle Jakob dead? Is that so? He was good to me. He was the only person I had in the world."

"Where were you living?"

"In Thurgau."

"Come with me."

"Certainly, Herr Studer."

"You know me? You've known me for some time?"

Ludwig said nothing. His eyes were wide open. The sergeant turned off the light and went out into the corridor. The young man followed him.

In the corridor on the floor below they ran into the innkeeper. Studer said, "I've brought another guest for you, Brönnimann. Have another bed put in my room, in Farny's room. Have you got that? And get the windowpane mended, I broke one."

"In the dead man's room? In the dead man's room. You can't mean it."

"I certainly do. He's not afraid. Are you, Ludwig?

"Of course not."

Brönnimann coughed, then wiped his reddened eyes with a handkerchief and stared at the young man. Contemptuously he said, "What d'you want with this poorhouse scum, Sergeant?"

Ludwig Farny went bright red and clenched his fists. Studer grasped his arm and pushed him into the room. "Keep calm, lad," he said quietly. "Just ignore the old man."

He thought – here he turned to Huldi – it would be more comfortable if Ludwig slept in his room. It wasn't healthy to spend the night on steel springs. You could catch your death of cold. While he spoke, Studer observed the girl and saw her blush. The colour suited her pale complexion well, he felt.

"Ludwig!" Huldi cried.

Now the lad blushed as well, embarrassment written all over his face.

"Er, yes," said Studer. "Is there anything wrong? I found him, and I'm keeping him with me. I need him, and that's that."

"But, Herr Studer! Don't you know that Ludwig knocked on my window last night – in the early morning, actually? He threw stones. The same night as our guest was murdered."

Ludwig bowed his head. Yes, that was right, he said. But what was wrong with that? And in a low voice he added that he knew nothing about the murder, nothing at all.

"We'll talk about that later," said Studer. "Would you leave us for the moment, Huldi? We've got some talking to do . . . haven't we, Ludwig?"

"Definitely, Herr Studer."

"Sit yourself down on the bed. I've got to look for something." Ludwig obeyed in silence.

Studer took the clothes out of the wardrobe: five pairs of pyjamas in raw silk, six elegant shirts, a dozen silk ties, underwear, silk and woollen socks, handkerchiefs. The Chinaman's camelhair smoking jacket was on a clothes hanger; beside it were two grey suits with the label of an English tailor and, finally, a fur-lined winter coat. Studer placed all these items of clothing neatly on the table and began to search the pockets. In the side pocket of the smoking jacket he found a letter:

Amriswil, 15 October

Deer Uncle – Deer Patron and Helper,

How are you and what are you doing? I hope you are stil in good health and feeling well. As I am. Now I will tel you how things have been going so far. From Gampligen I went to Zurich, I stayed there until the next Wednesday and looked for work. I didn't find any. I was compeled to go to Herisau on the 1st of August. I only stayed there for 2 weeks. It was a complete waste of time. After that I went to Amriswil. That's quite diferent. I have 13 beests to look after. 70 Fr in the summer, 60 in the winter, and enough work as I can do. They learned me to drive a tractor this summer. You don't have to rush about all the time, just press the peddles, but you have to watch what you're doing or it stops or goes too fast, but it's nice sitting at the steering wheel. I've been by myself up in the high meadows with the machine or the cart a lot and mown large bits. We also grow vegetables. I can give a hand there too. And another thing, I hope the horseshoes I dug up from under the lime tree will bring me luck, I went to the expense of buying a few lotery tickets, let's see if fortune will smile on me and that's all I have to tel.

Goodbye, dear Uncle, thank you for all your help. And warm regards from

Your Ludwig.

If you need me, just write to Amriswil.

The letter took up three sides of writing paper. On the fourth and last side the lad had written his address:

Herr Ludwig Farny,
Labourer,
Amriswil,
Thurgau Canton,
Switzerland,
Europe.

Studer was sitting in his favourite posture, elbows on his splayed thighs, with the letter in his hand. Of course. Not everyone knew that Amriswil was in Thurgau Canton, and it was not well known abroad

38

that Thurgau was part of Switzerland, and – better safe than sorry – if you had an uncle who liked to travel, then it was a good idea to point out that Switzerland was in Europe. The lad could not see the smile that was tugging at the corners of the Studer's lips, but, for the sergeant, the letter gave off a feeling of honesty, of decency that did him good. If his instinct was not deceiving him, Studer could cross Herr Ludwig Farny, Labourer from Amriswil, off his list of suspects for the murder. Anyway, he could always put it to the test . . .

"Ludwig," Studer called out. When the young man came over, he stuck the letter under his nose. "Did you write this?"

The lad had a curious way of blushing. First of all a flush rose up his throat, flooding his chin, cheeks and temples. Finally it reached his forehead, making his face look like one of those bizarre crustaceans that crawl around on the bottom of the sea and go deep red when thrown into boiling water.

"Yes, I did write to him. Anything wrong in that?"

"No, why ever should there be? But did your uncle reply?"

"You bet he did!"

"Show me the letter."

They were all the same, these farm labourers who didn't have much money. They didn't carry their wallet in the inside pocket of their jacket, like fine gentlemen, but in the lining of their waistcoat, inside, over their heart. It took some time, therefore, before Ludwig Farny had unbuttoned various articles of clothing and produced the battered wallet, which he had probably acquired by a swap. Ludwig extracted his uncle's reply from one of the compartments:

Pfründisberg, 15 November
Dear Ludwig,

I have only got round to answering your letter today. It would be good if you could give up your job in Amriswil immediately *and come here. I need you. Why, I will explain when you come. I presume you have enough money for the journey. I expect you on the 18th at the latest. You will live with me. As far as I can tell, someone is out to kill me. I trust you.*

    With best wishes,
    Uncle James

"Hm," said Studer, putting the letters next to each other on the table. "Your uncle wrote on the fifteenth. When did you get the letter?"

"The boss only gave it me on the seventeenth, at lunch. I grabbed a few things and set off. I got to Bern by that evening. I've a friend there and he lent me his bicycle. I rode off straight away, but it was about three in the morning by the time I got to Pfründisberg. I met one person on the road; he was on a motorbike and driving like hell. For a moment I thought I knew him, but then it wasn't who I thought it was. Huldi let me in, because I threw stones at her window, and let me sleep in her room – nothing happened between us!"

"Of course, of course – nothing happened between you."

"And now Huldi thinks I killed Uncle Jakob – probably because I arrived just after she heard the shot. I'm glad I've had the chance to talk to you, Herr Studer."

"Had the chance!" Studer growled. "Had the chance to talk to me! Do you think I didn't recognize you,

Ludwig? When was it I escorted you to the poorhouse? Three years ago? Two?" Studer had clasped his hands and was staring at the floor. Cold air was seeping in through the shattered windowpane. "Tell Huldi to come and light the stove, then bring a pot of glue and we can make the window draught-proof. Afterwards you can tell me your story."

The story of Barbara

The broken windowpane had been patched up, the stove was drawing nicely, the crackle of wood came from it. Studer looked at his watch – only half past five. In an hour's time Studer intended to pay a visit to Hungerlott, the poorhouse warden.

"Right then, Ludwig," said Studer after he had offered him a Brissago. The detective sergeant and his guest were puffing away.

It was a simple story. Ludwig had never known his father and had taken his mother's name. When he was six, his mother had married a bricklayer called Äbi. The marriage had produced two children, a girl called Anna, who later married Hungerlott, and a boy, Ernst, who would graduate – graduate, the lad said, not gradate! – from the horticultural college at the end of the year.

"My stepfather didn't want me at home, so my mother sent me to some relatives out in the country, two old spinsters. They were both in the Salvation Army, Martha and Erika, and I had to go to the meetings with them on Sundays. But then Erika got ill. I don't know whether you've come across that kind of thing: it wasn't a physical illness; she refused to speak and crept round the house not saying a word. Eventually some women came to fetch her. They said she'd tried to hang herself out in the woods.

"After that Mother didn't want me to stay with Martha any longer, so I was put into service with a farmer . . . Herding the goats. Mucking out the cow-shed. On Sundays the farmer went to the inn, and since he had no children, he beat me when he got home. I think," a faint smile crossing Ludwig's lips, "he would have liked to beat his wife, but she was stronger than him, so he took it out on me. It's not nice when you get beaten every Sunday, Herr Studer, and during the week as well, when you never get any fun the whole year through and your mother doesn't even come to see you at Christmas. I was twelve years old. I was hungry. I stole a bit of cheese here, a bit of meat there – just because I was hungry. I think the farmer would have been happy to ignore it, he was glad to have someone he could hit. But his wife was stingy, and she reported me to the mayor, so I was dumped in the reformatory. You can take it from me that that wasn't very nice either, Herr Studer. Later on I read newspapers a lot, and once I found an illustrated magazine with a picture of our reformatory. We looked fine in the magazine, but I never learned much that was any use there. They all said I was too stupid, the instructors and the principal, but I'm not specially stupid, Herr Studer . . . I know I make spelling mistakes, but it's not that terrible to make a spelling mistake, is it? So I had to help on the farm. I liked that. I like animals, cows, goats, horses. Eventually I was released, and I looked for work. Believe me, Herr Studer, I wasn't asking for much. Just my work and my wages, that's all, but then I fell ill, once in the winter, and it affected my lungs. I was spitting blood, always tired, sweating during the night – the doctor sent me to a sanatorium. For two years! When I came out I'd forgotten everything I'd learned. I tried to work for a farmer, but he threw me out after two days, saying I was useless. So the government sent me to Pfründisberg, to the poorhouse. You

43

know, I sometimes thought that was worse than prison. The director, or rather, the warden is very good at giving lectures on pau . . ."

"Pauperism," Studer interjected.

"Exactly. Pauperism. But the only thing you really learn there is how to drink schnapps . . ."

There was something harrowing about the simple way he told his story, and Studer had a soft heart. He felt beads of sweat running down his cheeks. At first he blamed the overheated stove, but only for a moment, then he realized it was Ludwig's story that was bringing the tears to his eyes. "Is there much more?" he asked in a hoarse voice. "I mean, of your story?"

"No, Herr Studer." What a gentle voice the lad had! "I'd just like to tell you about Barbara. Barbara was a bit lame. Otherwise she was like Huldi. The same broad face, you know, the same pale skin and the same brown plaits. Barbara was in the poorhouse too. I could only see her on Sundays. We'd go for walks in the woods together, and she'd tell me about her home. She hadn't had a nice time of it either. One Sunday evening we met one of the female warders on the way back, and Barbara said she didn't want to go back to the poorhouse any more, they'd all tease her because she'd been out with me. I tried to calm her down, but it was no use. You know the proverb, Herr Studer, you've made your bed, now you must lie on it. When I realized Barbara wasn't going back to the poorhouse, we went off together. It was six o'clock in the evening. On the third of June. I remember it so well because the warden drove past in his car, but he didn't recognize us, just drove on. We walked and walked. Sometimes Barbara couldn't walk any longer, so I carried her . . . We came to the Jura, the part where they speak French, and the farmers were better there. I got work –

in the mountains they don't start making the hay until the middle of July. I would always go first myself, work for the day, then explain that my wife was with me. Lots of the farmers said I should just bring her along, she could help in the house. Barbara was a good worker; sometimes we stayed a whole week in the same place. But we had no papers, and without papers you're lost in this world. They're not interested in the people and whether they're hardworking and honest, all they're interested in is whether they've got a brown booklet with a photo, with stamps and signatures . . .

"Then autumn came – it comes quickly in the mountains. So this is what we did: as soon as the willows were ready for cutting, I gathered them and we wove baskets, Barbara and me, and sold them in the villages. Usually *I* was the one who went, since Barbara couldn't walk far. She stayed at home . . . Home! A woodcutter's hut in the middle of the forest. We'd saved some money during the summer, so we had enough to buy pots and blankets for the winter; we had wood aplenty, and there was a stream quite close to the hut. The hut was always clean, and we lived there as man and wife, Herr Studer.

"But in February Barbara fell ill – and it was an illness I knew. She sweated during the night, she coughed and brought up blood. I looked after her as well as I could; we slept on pine twigs, but it didn't help. At the end of April she died.

"Where should I go? My world had fallen apart. So I thought I might as well go back to Pfründisberg. I was in no hurry. I took work here and there, so it was July before I got back, on the eighteenth, to be precise. It was six o'clock in the morning when I arrived in Pfründisberg, and the first person I saw was Huldi. Did I tell you that Barbara and Huldi had been at school together? Huldi took me in, gave me something to eat and went to the poorhouse and put in a good word for me with the warden. Hungerlott threw a fit. He bawled at me, said he'd inform the police, I didn't belong in Pfründisberg any more, I should be in another place where they were stricter. But while he was making all this fuss in the courtyard, a gentleman suddenly appeared. He had a snow-white moustache coming down over the corners of his mouth and he spoke formal German. He asked Hungerlott what all the noise was about.

" 'That bastard Farny, the scum, he ran away and now he has the cheek to come back.'

" 'Farny?' the old gentleman asked. He started talking to me and it turned out this fine gentleman was my uncle, my mother's brother. That shut Hungerlott up. My uncle found me a job in Thurgau, gave me money to get there, and so off I went . . .

"If only I'd stayed here," Ludwig sighed, rubbing his eyes with the ball of his thumb.

Studer cleared his throat. "And Huldi?" he asked.

"But I told you, Herr Studer. Huldi and Barbara were in the same class . . ."

"So now Huldi's your girlfriend?"

Again the flush spread up from his neck over his chin, cheeks, temples and forehead. Embarrassed, the lad mumbled, "Uncle would've quite liked us to get married."

The sergeant stood up and raised his broad hand, letting it fall on Ludwig's back.

"Lucky devil," he said. "So that's agreed, then. You'll help me solve this case."

"Pauperism"

The odd couple – Sergeant Studer with his broad shoulders in his grey, off-the-peg suit, and Ludwig Farny in his rustic linen-mixture jacket and trousers – had dinner. They had stewed pork in a creamy sauce with rösti, and the ex-farm labourer consumed vast quantities.

"You stay in the room, Ludwig," said Studer once the dishes had been cleared away. "I have a visit to make. You're responsible for the room. You're not to let anyone in. Understood?"

"Yes, Studer," said Ludwig, and you could see that he would resolutely carry out the defence with which he had been entrusted. And the sergeant was glad he had simply said "Studer" and not "Herr".

The mist had cleared, and there was frost on the ground. Thin banks of cloud drifted across the sky, hiding the moon, then releasing it again. It was small and green, like an unripe lemon – it was just like the moon on that July night.

The poorhouse was in a former monastery that had been adapted to take in the poor and needy. The puddles in the streets to the poorhouse had thin layers of ice. Studer came into a courtyard that was dark. A paved path led to a door with the reddish glow of a light bulb over it. The sergeant went in – and felt like turning round and going straight out again as the smell in the vestibule hit him, almost taking his breath away. It smelled of poverty, it smelled of dirt. Muffled sounds could be heard behind a door on the left. Studer went over and opened it without knocking.

Three steps led down into a dungeon-like room. Bare bulbs dangled from the ceiling, illuminating tables with thick wooden tops at which men in grubby blue overalls sat. A man was walking up and down between the tables – presumably the guard on duty. Studer entered unnoticed, shut the door behind him and stood on the second step. On the table in front of the men were billycans and tin bowls. There was a smell of chicory coffee and thin soup. There was another smell mixed in with it: the smell of damp clothes, of underwear.

The men sat there, their forearms on the table, as if they had to erect a wall to protect their billycan of coffee and bowl of soup. Now and then one of the walls formed by the arms would open up, and a hand would go through to steal a piece of bread. A quarrel would flare up, and the warder had to come over and restore the peace. Eventually the peacemaker became aware of the massive figure of the sergeant. A few quick strides brought him over to the steps, and in a harsh voice he demanded to know what he wanted.

He had to speak to the warden, Studer said.

Anyone could say that, the warder replied. Without a word, Studer took his identification out of his wallet and stuck it under the man's nose.

The change in the warder was remarkable. He forced his lips into an obsequious smile, he even tried to sweeten the harshness of his voice as he said, "Herr Hungerlott will be delighted . . ." He opened the door, stepping aside to let Studer through first. Behind them, all hell broke loose. Some of them chanted the chorus he'd heard five months ago: "We don't want any cops in Pfründisberg . . ."

"Order!" the warder shouted. "Behave yourselves until I'm back, or there'll be trouble." But his warning was drowned in the uproar. The noise of the unsupervised men could be heard through the door.

Corridors . . . long corridors. Occasionally the walls were interrupted by a window, and you could see how thick the walls were. Steps . . . corridors . . . nooks and crannies . . . It was a labyrinth you'd have certainly got lost in without a guide.

And then they reached the new part of the poor-house. The corridors had inlaid linoleum as well as coconut matting, which dampened the noise of their footsteps . . . A door. Below the bell-pull was a brass plate with a name in fancy lettering: *Vinzenz Hungerlott-Äbi, Warden*. The warder pulled the bell, a simple action that was full of respect, of obsequiousness. They could hear the bell ringing in the apartment, and a girl came to open the door. She was smartly dressed, with a white lace apron standing out against the black of her dress. Breathless, the warder announced, "Sergeant . . . Studer . . . would . . . like to speak to the warden." The maid disappeared and returned with an invitation to the sergeant to step in. The warder bade Studer such a polite farewell, he wondered what the man had to hide.

But he did not have long to pursue this reflection, for when he entered the warden's study he found a surprise waiting for him. A man got up from the depths of a leather armchair, a man Studer had certainly not expected to find here: his billiards partner, Münch, the lawyer. As always, he was wearing a high wing collar and was twisting and craning his neck. Hungerlott was sitting at the desk. He stood up and said, "Very nice of you to come, Sergeant. As I can see, you know my friend Münch . . ."

Yes, yes, said Studer dryly, he'd known Münch for a long time. He was, however, surprised to find him here.

"There's a very good reason, which will become apparent," said Hungerlott in his lecturing tone. "You wouldn't have dreamed four months ago that we would meet again under such tragic circumstances, would you, Sergeant?"

Studer felt embarrassed, a feeling he hated. He really ought to offer this Hungerlott his condolences because he'd lost his wife.

"Please do be seated, Sergeant. Perhaps here, opposite your friend Münch? Beside the fire? I should tell you that the central heating does not work very well here. That is why I have a little fire lit in the evening. It's warm and bright and cosy . . . is it not, Münch?"

"I must offer you my condolences," said Studer, "for the grievous . . ." He didn't get any farther. The lawyer from Bern had grasped the opportunity, while the warden was busy selecting the drinks, to give the sergeant a kick on the shin. Studer accepted it without a murmur, although he had no idea what the reason behind it was.

"Yes," said Herr Hungerlott, "it was a grievous loss. And so sudden."

"And what did Frau Hungerlott . . .?" Again the kick on the shin. Studer thanked God he had put his leather gaiters on. Naturally he could not ask his friend the lawyer why he was dispensing kicks, but there must be some reason for it.

"You were wondering what my wife died of? A particularly virulent form of gastric influenza. Dr Buff was tireless – beyond the call of duty – but he could not save her."

The looks the lawyer was giving him were eloquent,

and Studer could read them without difficulty. They said, "What are you doing getting involved in this? What has the death of Frau Hungerlott to do with you? Oh, Studer," the looks said, "why must you always ask silly questions and end up with egg on your face?"

"What would you like, gentlemen?" Hungerlott asked. "Wine? Beer? Brandy?"

Münch answered for his friend. "If you don't mind, Warden, we'll both have a small brandy."

In the silence the sound of the cork being drawn could clearly be heard. The golden liquid with the sharp aroma glug-glugged into the glasses. Why did the sergeant recall the crystal glasses on that July night when the Chinaman balanced on the back legs of his chair, his leather slippers dangling from his toes?

"*Prost*," said Herr Hungerlott. He was standing between the two friends and clinked glasses first with the sergeant, then with the lawyer. He was wearing a suit of dark-grey cloth; the jacket was cut like a tunic and buttoned up to the neck; a tie appeared under his collar, emerald green with red spots. The tie could be seen only when Herr Hungerlott turned his head to one side, otherwise his goatee concealed the vibrant splash of colour.

"Pauperism, the scientific study of poverty." The warden of the Pfründisberg poorhouse was launching into a lecture.

"We know a lot about poverty. We know, for example, that there are people who will never get on in the world. It is not their fault. I would almost say – at the risk of being considered superstitious – that these people are predestined to remain poor, that it is in their stars . . ."

A lecture continued

Hungerlott walked up and down, his hands deep in his trouser pockets. His steps were soundless, the floor was covered with a thick carpet. Beside the window was a huge desk in solid wood. The top was empty – and Studer was reminded of the table in the room of the murdered Chinaman. Beech logs crackled in the fireplace. They gave off a bright flame, just looking at them made you feel warm. Opposite the sergeant, in a comfortable leather armchair, was Münch, his right leg crossed over his left. Studer had adopted his favourite posture, elbows on his splayed thighs, hands clasped, and was staring at the fire. Two of the walls were covered in shelves, and as the sergeant let the lecture flow over him, he ran his eye along the spines of the books from a distance. Among them he found old friends: Gross, *Handbook for Examining Magistrates*, books by Locard, Lombrosos Rhodes, and two shelves were filled with crime novels: Agatha Christie, Anthony Berkeley, Simenon . . .

"They can't even organize their lives, financially, I mean, everything they touch seems to fall apart, they find it impossible to retain a job, and if they happen to have inherited money from their parents, they manage to lose it – and not through their own fault: a bank collapses, a lawyer is dishonest – that is not a dig at you, my dear Münch."

"I should hope not," the lawyer growled, sticking his index finger inside his collar.

"You see how touchy people are, Studer. I tried to explain my theory of pauperism to the government – pauperism as fate, not as fault – but I was not given a hearing. And yet every day I could find proof of my theory. If you only knew, Studer, how many lives go through my hands. I have had people sent to Pfründisberg simply because they were unemployed! I go to great pains to help these people – the curse is the community in which they have to live. You can have no idea, Studer, how great an influence their environment has. Ten boozers and layabouts can infect a hundred decent people. And the problem is that we have ten boozers and layabouts. It is in vain that I have attempted to persuade the authorities to remove these elements. In vain! The only answer I get is: these people have committed no crime, they have simply fallen on hard times through no fault of their own. It is the duty of the Poor Board to help these unfortunates. You can judge for yourself, Studer: for each of our inmates we get one franc, seventeen rappen per day; and that has to cover everything: food, clothing, the doctor. How can I manage on that? I can't even give them decent food, and I'm sure you'll agree that poor food affects the mind as well as the body. I do everything possible . . ."

"And buy yourself a car," thought Studer.

There were many things the sergeant disliked about Herr Hungerlott. First of all there were the two rings welded into one on his ring finger – his late wife's ring soldered onto his own; all the time Herr Hungerlott kept playing with this double ring, which was far too big for his skinny fingers. Secondly, there was his goatee. His cheeks were smooth-shaven, only on his chin was there a proliferation of hair, its colour a dirty greyish brown. And, thirdly, there was Herr Hungerlott's strange suit with its buttonup jacket and his colourful tie that peeked out only from time to time. Then, fourthly and lastly, the warden said "Studer" and not "Herr Studer". But there was one thing he definitely liked about the man: he loved to hear himself speak. Since Sergeant Studer himself preferred to remain silent, he had nothing against people who liked to hear themselves speak. It meant he could sit quietly in his chair, let the words flow over him and stare into the fire . . .

But what the devil did those two kicks mean that his friend, the lawyer, had bestowed on him? Studer stole a glance at Münch out of the corner of his eye, but he was far too occupied with his too-high wing collar, which was rubbing the skin on his neck.

"I do everything possible," Herr Hungerlott continued his lecture, "but I find myself in a dilemma, and there is no way out that I can see: on the one hand, it is my duty as warden of a poorhouse to teach those in my care the love of work, to convince them that it is only through work that they will be able to return to an ordered existence. On the other hand, there is my personal conviction, my belief, one might almost say, that poverty is the destiny of certain people and that nothing can change the course their life will take, not work, not effort, not devotion to duty."

"It was gastric influenza Frau Hungerlott died of?" Studer asked. He kept staring at the fire, not deigning to glance at Herr Hungerlott.

The third kick! Studer did not move a muscle.

"Of . . . yes . . . of gastric influenza . . . that is correct, a particularly virulent form of gastric influenza," the warden stammered.

"And did James Farny leave a will?" Studer asked impassively.

The lawyer clasped his hands and looked to the heavens in despair. What was his friend Studer up to?

"I think . . . How do you mean, Herr Studer? Of course he made a will. He left his estate to his relatives . . . To his sister – my mother-in-law, heh heh, who's married to a very dubious character in Bern.

"Well, perhaps dubious character's going too far. After all, Arnold Äbi is my father-in-law. But before I married Anna, the Poor Board twice proposed Äbi should be put away. He's a drunkard, he used to be a bricklayer, but now he's somewhat work-shy – I think I may say that, even though I am related to him. Apart from my mother-in-law, my wife comes into the reckoning as an heir. She's dead now, and I don't know exactly what will happen in that case. Anna's brother will inherit too. His name is Ernst, and he is taking the one-year course at the horticultural college. In connection with that, I feel I should point out that James Farny paid for his nephew's course and also kept him supplied with pocket money, while my wife did not receive one rappen – I repeat, not one rappen – from her uncle. That is why I wanted to ask my friend Münch's advice. The sums that were paid to Ernst Äbi should be deducted from his inheritance as a matter of course, should they not? Apart from these, there is one other person who bears the name of Farny: an illegitimate child of Frau Äbi, whose maiden name was Farny, which she naturally gave to the child. Who the father was, no one knows. Whether this Ludwig Farny is also a legal heir" – "He is," Münch growled, but the warden pretended he didn't hear and went on – "is something for the courts to decide. After discussing the matter with my friend Münch, I will appoint an attorney to look after my interests . . ."

Studer stood up, stretched and yawned uninhibitedly. "That will be all for this evening, *Herr* Hungerlott," he said, emphasizing the word "Herr" – indeed, he even added an emphatic movement of his hand. He shook hands with neither of the others but strode to the door, picked up his coat in the hall and, since he had a good sense of direction, managed to find the way out.

He went back to the Sun Inn. The light was still on in the bar, but the sergeant felt a need for solitude. So he made his way to the room where James Farny had been murdered. A second bed had been made up. In it Ludwig Farny, farm labourer from Amriswil, was sleeping the sleep of the just: that is, he was snoring outrageously. The sergeant gave him a clip round the ear. The lad shot up, startled, his dishevelled straw-blond hair sticking out and the blue of his eyes shining, shining . . .

Grumpily, the sergeant said to his protégé, "If you're going to snore like that, I won't be able to sleep."

"I'm sorry, Herr Studer, but I always snore when I'm tired."

"Then lie on your side. Lying on your back always makes you snore."

Obediently Ludwig turned his face to the wall, and in less than a minute was fast asleep once more. Two minutes later the snoring started again, sounding like the rasp of a lumberjack's saw. Studer undressed, muttering curses to himself, then, in his flannel pyjamas and leather slippers, he inspected the room once more. The walls were wood-panelled; the sergeant examined each plank – but he found nothing. At last, since he was getting cold, he crept into bed. As he was dropping off, he mumbled to himself, "Farny certainly wasn't shot in this room, otherwise I'd have found the bullet."

For a few minutes his assistant's snoring kept him awake, but then he grew accustomed to it and fell asleep, peacefully, his lean head lying on his right hand.

The third locale

When, in later years, Studer told the story of James Farny, he also called it the story of the three locales. "For," he would say, "the case of the Chinaman took place in three locales: in a village inn, in a poorhouse, in a horticultural college. That's why I sometimes call it the story of the three locales."

The next morning it was the turn of the third locale, the horticultural college. First of all Studer had breakfast with Ludwig Farny, the assistant chance had brought him, then he set off with him to pay a visit to the principal, Sack-Amherd. He felt an urge to make the acquaintance of Ernst Äbi, the Chinaman's other nephew.

There had been a change in the weather during the night; the *Föhn* was blowing. The slope on the other side of the valley stood out clearly; the leaves of individual birches shone like gold coins in the sun, and the deciduous wood was a crimson glow in its frame of dark-green pines.

As soon as he entered the grounds of the horticultural college, he could see that things were different there. Although the gravel had been scraped up into heaps – so that it wouldn't be trodden into the soil during the damp winter months – it was obvious that the paths had been laid on a bed of stone. In the distance the hum of a rotary hoe could be heard; along a stone wall was an orchard of dwarf fruit trees in which a group of students stood. Studer's arrival caused some agitation among them; he thought he could hear whispers and chatter. But he continued to stride forward undeterred – fifty yards – thirty yards – then he heard a voice he knew: "Pay attention. There's nothing to see over there. This is a lesson. Now here you have to be careful."

Studer recognized the speaker: the principal, Herr Sack-Amherd, was wearing a fur-lined coat – the collar was fur too, as was his hat – and his hands were in lined leather gloves. He was wearing galoshes over his shoes, and his trousers were immaculately ironed. In his hand he had a gleaming pair of nickel-plated secateurs with which he snipped off a twig here and there.

"For the dwarf pyramid the most important thing is to avoid damaging the structure, the shape of the tree. Of course there are gardeners who chop away anything that comes to hand. I don't call that pruning, I call it botching ... Ah! Good morning, Herr Studer. Delighted to see you again. You'll be here about the murder, of course. I hope you don't suspect one of our students ... do you?"

Studer shook his slim hand, muttered some vague greeting and drew the principal to one side, away from the staring students.

"Naturally I want to cause your college as little disruption as possible, Principal," he said. "But I will have to question at least one of your students, that much is unavoidable. I have been told he is a nephew of the murdered man. Ernst Äbi they say he's called. I think it will even be necessary to search his locker ..."

"To search his locker! You don't say! To search the locker of one of my students! – Äbi!" he called out, and his voice cracked.

How old could this student be? Certainly older than

the others. Twenty-six? Twenty-eight? An old acquaintance as well. It was the student with such a long nose it looked like a caricature. When the student reached the two men, the principal barked at him, "Nothing but trouble we have with you. Now the police want to search your locker. Can you imagine what that does for the college's reputation?"

Was he imagining things? It seemed to the sergeant that Ernst Äbi had gone pale. But Studer deliberately put on a genial voice when he said, "Let's make it like at the dentist's, Herr Sack-Amherd, the quicker the better."

Giving Ludwig a signal to keep an eye on his stepbrother, he led the way, together with the principal, to the college.

It was a broad building, in the mixture of styles favoured by the canton architect: part farm, part village school, part factory building. The main door decorated with ornamental metalwork. Inside, they came into a square hall from which a staircase with a double turn went up to the first floor. In the space between the two flights was a little moss-grown fountain surrounded by a few potted chrysanthemums with stems between one and three feet high. The flowers were colourful, bronze, crimson, gold – and white. As Studer went up the stairs with the principal, he turned around. The scene he saw was to haunt him for a long time.

Ludwig Farny had placed his broad, calloused hand on his stepbrother's shoulder. There was a worried look in those eyes with their remarkable blue sheen. The young labourer's protective gesture – he was much smaller than his stepbrother – was so touching that Studer felt a momentary pang of conscience. But he had a job to do, after all. You can't let yourself be swayed by feelings in an investigation.

If the sergeant thought he was going to be taken straight to Ernst Äbi's locker, he was mistaken. Even a murder is not enough to keep the principal of a college from showing off the glories of his establishment. Moreover, Herr Sack-Amherd suffered from asthma. So he took his visitor on a guided tour of the whole of the first floor, giving him the opportunity to admire the sickbay (it had two beds), the library, the museum, the conference room. As they entered the last-named, it suddenly occurred to the principal that he had forgotten to get another teacher to stand in for him. At first he was going to send Äbi, but the sergeant protested. So Ludwig was sent, and Studer had to wait in the room, in which a table covered in green baize was looking bored, despite the presence of six high-backed chairs round it.

"Off you go, lad," said Herr Sack-Amherd, describing the shortest way. "Tell him I'll be occupied until eleven. He's to take the rest to the glasshouse and give them a lesson on pot plants. Wottli's his name. His nameplate's on the letter box. You've got that?"

Again Ludwig blushed and glanced at his stepbrother, who was leaning with his forehead against the window and staring out into the garden. Then he left. In order to free himself from the principal's chatter, Studer sat down and leafed through a book that was on the table. It was a strange book. An Indian had written it, and it described bizarre experiments. With the help of complicated instruments, the author had measured the plants' pulse, which he had managed to slow down with injections of chloroform and speed up with injections of caffeine . . .

Eventually Ludwig Farny returned, and the four of them went up to the second floor. Here, too, Studer had to admire the dormitories, their gleaming parquet floors, the iron bedsteads painted white, with eider-downs and pillows in red-checked covers. Then, finally, the group went out into the corridor (the grey tiles had a coconut-matting runner, and the washroom had two dozen white porcelain basins with hot and cold taps) and stopped by a locker with the number 26 painted in black on it.

"Open it," the principal commanded. Turning to the sergeant, he added, "Naturally I have a second key for every locker, but it seems to me . . ."

Ernst Äbi opened his locker. Work clothes, a Sunday suit . . . underwear, shoes . . . Studer started to clear it out, placing every object neatly on the coconut matting. From time to time he threw a sidelong glance at Ernst Äbi and marvelled at the paleness of the tip of the lad's nose. A vague memory of the book he had just leafed through came to mind: he would have liked to feel the horticultural student's pulse, to see if it was beating faster. People probably didn't need a toxic substance, as plants did, to speed up the circulation of blood . . .

"What's this?" Studer had taken the shoes out and now he was holding a package, tied up with string, and weighing it suspiciously in his hand. "What's this?" he repeated.

No answer. Ernst Äbi had put on a stubborn expression. So the sergeant untied the knot, removed the paper and looked at what came to light.

A pair of raw-silk pyjamas. A spattering of red on the trousers . . . but the jacket was covered in blood. There was a frayed hole on the left-hand side of the front.

"What's this?" Studer asked for the third time. When the student still refused to answer, the principal lost his temper: "Will you answer?!"

But Ernst Äbi had his lips clamped between his

teeth, and not only the tip of his nose was pale; his whole face was. Ludwig Farny, on the other hand, had gone bright red and was staring anxiously at his stepbrother.

Studer tried once more: "Where did you find this, Ernstli?"

Again the obstinate silence. His friendly approach was getting him nowhere, so Studer dropped the blood-stained pyjamas on the floor, went over to the window with the wrapping paper and examined it . . . No doubt about it, the address that had been on it had been scratched out with a penknife. However, if he held the paper up to the window, the letters could be clearly seen:

Herr Paul Wottli, Instructor, Horticultural College, Pfründisberg bei Gampligen. And the sender: *Frau Emilie Wottli, 25 Aarbergergasse, Bern.*

It could be a clue. The well-fed principal of the college had stared at Studer's every action. Had Herr Studer found something? he wanted to know, as he fiddled with the white-gold watch chain dangling over his paunch. The sergeant said nothing, just shrugged his shoulders.

Wottli . . . Wottli . . . He had the feeling he'd heard the name. Hadn't Ludwig been sent to see a Wottli? Wasn't Wottli the name of the teacher who'd had to stand in for the principal?

"What are your teachers' names, Herr Direktor?"

Sack-Amherd held up his right hand and dutifully counted off the members of staff:

"Blumenstein, he does fruit-growing, Kehrli does vegetables and Wottli does pot plants; he also teaches composting and chemistry. Wottli's a very capable teacher, that's why I had him take over my class."

"Is Wottli married?"

"No, Sergeant. He looks after his mother, and she lives in Bern. A good son – a model son." How sweet the principal's voice sounded! His lips formed a perfect circle: "Oh yes, Wottli will go far. Incidentally, my teacher" – *my* teacher, the fat man said – "was also very friendly with the late Herr Farny. I wouldn't be surprised if Wottli received a legacy ... He was very rich, you know, though a bit of an eccentric, writing his memoirs in an out-of-the-way inn."

So Herr Sack-Amherd also knew that the Chinaman was writing his memoirs.

"Have you read his memoirs, Herr Direktor?"

"Only in part. Once Herr Farny read out from them to us."

Studer suddenly turned to Äbi: "Where did you find the wrapping paper?"

Silence, obstinate silence. Ludwig Farny tried to get his stepbrother to speak.

"Come on, Ernst, tell us," he said, begging, imploring him. His voice seemed to tremble with tears.

But Ernst Äbi refused to speak. He shrugged his shoulders, raising them so high they touched his ears, which were big and very red, as if to suggest by that gesture that it was pointless to say anything. And the sergeant could understand his mute protest ...

"If you have no objection, Herr Sack-Amherd," (Studer used his best formal German for this suggestion) "then perhaps we could – with your approval, of course, only if *you* have no objection – come to the following conclusion: you yourself will have to admit that the discovery of this strangely suspicious package suggests your student is guilty of – or at least implicated in the mysterious murder ..."

"Mysterious, very mysterious," Sack-Amherd sighed, slipping into Swiss dialect.

"Do you know what? On the first floor you have a splendid sickbay, which is empty, completely empty, proof of how hygienically run your school is . . ."

Flattered, Sack-Amherd laughed, modestly digging his chin into the black cravat covering his starched shirtfront.

"I don't want to arrest Ernst Äbi until I'm absolutely sure," Studer went on, speaking loudly enough for the two stepbrothers to hear every syllable. "How would it be if we put the pair of them into the sickbay? Then Ludwig Farny could keep an eye on his stepbrother, and I would be sure he wouldn't try to escape. I trust Ludwig Farny . . ."

"What?" the principal hissed, sticking his chin out. "What? You trust him, a former inmate of the poorhouse? A man who's been in and out of reformatories?"

"Yes," said Studer mildly, "I trust him because the Chin– er, his uncle also trusted him."

"On *your* responsibility, Herr Studer. And if the police will cover you, I have no . . ."

"OK, Ludwig?" The lad nodded. "And you, Ernst?"

"Yes . . . fine."

"That's that, then." Studer gave a sigh of satisfaction. "As far as I'm concerned, they can have the freedom of the building during the day, but at six you, Principal, will lock them in the sickbay and keep the key until the morning. I am making you responsible for your student."

Sack-Amherd was about to protest, but then he desisted and nodded to indicate his agreement.

"Goodbye, one and all." The sergeant waved his hand, gently ruffled his assistant's straw-blond hair, then crooked his finger and gave Ernst Äbi a friendly tap on the chest. "And you, clodhopper, don't do anything silly."

Then he slowly went down the stairs. He could still hear the principal's angry voice. Sack-Amherd was annoyed at the expression "clodhopper". The word was an insult for a student who was due to receive his diploma from the college next February.

Old Mother Trili

The route from the horticultural college to the Sun Inn led past the entrance to the poorhouse courtyard. The sergeant stopped in the gateway and watched an old woman doing washing in a large wooden tub. Matted, grey-white hair fluttered round a tiny little head, her nose had been pushed over to the right and had huge nostrils. On the ground beside her were dirty sheets, shirts, pillowcases, handkerchiefs, and a young cockerel was strutting round her feet, occasionally attempting to crow. The young rooster never quite managed it, the laborious cock-a-doodle-doo cracked in the middle – presumably the creature's voice was just breaking.

"Good day to you, Mother." Studer stopped and stuck his hands deep in his coat pockets. His right elbow was pressing the package he had found in Ernst Äbi's locker to his hip.

"And to you, handsome fellow." The old woman giggled, then coughed, winking at him with watery eyes.

"Hard at it?"

"What d'you think? Naught but work for Old Mother Trili, work, work, work."

Three inmates in faded blue overalls were shuffling slowly, like bears, across the yard. Each had a besom and was brushing up the dust – but a sudden gust of wind came and scattered the pile they'd swept up. Then the brooms started once more scratching at the stamped earth.

Had Old Mother Trili always had to slave away like this? the sergeant asked. Presumably she'd had less work when Frau Hungerlott was still alive?

Her? Her get her hands wet? With her painted fingernails? The warden's wife never came near any soapsuds. It was Old Mother Trili who'd always had to do the washing. "And that's a fact, ain't it, Hansli?"

The cockerel stretched and twisted its neck – just like Münch trying to get comfortable in his too-high wing collar, Studer thought – then laid its crimson comb to one side and blinked. "*Cocka-oo-oo*," it said, which in its language presumably expressed its agreement with the old woman.

Then the cockerel ran across the yard, stopped at one of the piles of dust, scratched, pecked. The three inmates watched it, leaning on the handles of their besoms. Then they felt in their pockets and threw it crumbs of bread.

"Hansli!" the washerwoman called. The cock trotted over, tried to crow, shook itself and began to peck at the sheets lying on the ground. Old Mother Trili sang a folk song:

In my granny's chamber there blows a hmhmhm,
In my granny's chamber there blows a sharp wind.
I shiver and quiver all from the hmhmhm,
I shiver and quiver all from the sharp wind.
You take the begging bowl, I'll take the hmhmhm,
You take the begging bowl, I'll take the sack.

While Studer was wondering why the old woman was singing an Appenzell song instead of a Bernese one, he suddenly felt the package, which he held clasped under his elbow, fall to the ground. It broke open and the blood-soaked pyjamas shone in the sun, which came out between two clouds. At first the cockerel fluttered backwards in alarm, but then it came closer, dug its claws in the thin material and pecked and pecked, just as it had been doing at the dirty bed linen.

"Shoo, shoo! . . . Get away, will you?" The sergeant clapped his hands, but the cockerel just stood there and let out another "*Cocka-oo-oo*".

"That's a tame cockerel you've got there," said Studer, astonished.

"You are, aren't you, Hansli? We understand each other, you and me." The old woman took some washing out of the tub, wrung it out and dropped it on the cobbles beside her. Studer bent down to pick up his package, but the bird had got quite excited. It jumped up and down, tearing at the paper with its beak. Then it let go and went back to pecking at the dust.

Finally Studer managed to wrap the pyjamas up in the brown paper again. Then he told the old woman she had a good voice for her age and asked her what the Frau Hungerlott's illness had been like.

Old Mother Trili slapped her hand into the soapsuds – a dab of lather landed on the end of Studer's thin nose. "Cruel it was, the way she had to suffer, poor Frau Hungerlott," she said and sniffed. Then she rubbed her eyes with the back of her wet hand.

"Cruel?" Studer asked. "What kind of an illness was it?"

Now the old woman clapped her right hand over her mouth. There had been something not right about it, she said, but it was best to hold your tongue.

What had been mysterious about it, Studer wanted to know, and why wasn't she to say anything?

You were always better off if you didn't talk too much, she said.

The sergeant nodded. That was all well and good, he

said, but she could trust him. She could rely on him not to go telling other people. A detective knew when to keep his mouth shut.

But that assurance did not seem to make much impression on the old woman. She hummed her song:

You take the begging bowl, I'll take the hmhmhm,
You take the begging bowl, I'll take the sack.

Hardly had she finished than something strange happened. The cockerel, that had pecked around in the dirty washing and had a go at Studer's find with its pointed beak, fell down. Its eyelid came up over its eye, it gave a weak "*cocka–*," stretched out its claws – and died.

The old woman broke out into lamentation: "Hansli, my little Hansli! What's happened to you?"

The tears tumbled down out of her red-rimmed eyes. She picked the bird up and cradled it in her arms like a little baby, giving the sergeant reproachful looks, as if she thought he was responsible for the cockerel's death. The three other inmates stood round Old Mother Trili, leaning on their brooms, one behind her, one to the right and one to the left. Studer was reminded of the scene that had greeted him at the graveyard when he arrived the previous day. Three men standing round a dead body.

How surprisingly quickly the cockerel had died. The sergeant remembered that the bird had pecked at the dirty washing lying beside the washtub, so he bent down started to look through the pile. Three handkerchiefs. They smelled unpleasantly of garlic. He turned each one over and over until he had found the monogram: two intertwined letters, A. Ä. – Anna Äbi . . .

Garlic? It didn't prove much. Anyway, the cockerel had also had its beak in the package he now had clamped under his elbow. So he lifted that to his nose as well. No doubt about it, the brown paper also smelled of garlic ... A vague recollection of the investigation into a poisoning came back to mind. In that case sheets and handkerchiefs had been tested and his friend at the Institute for Forensic Medicine, Dr Malapelle from Milan, had explained that a smell of garlic almost always indicated the presence of arsenic; and if the Marsh test produced a black arsenic mirror, he had gone on, then you had all the proof you needed ... Anna Hungerlott-Äbi ... Her handkerchiefs in the dirty washing smelled of garlic ... but the brown paper addressed to a certain Herr Wottli also smelled of garlic ... Wottli – a teacher at Pfründisberg Horticultural College.

Confusion reigned in Studer's mind: the Chinaman's body had been lying on the grave of Anna Hungerlott-Äbi; his coat, jacket and waistcoat had been undamaged and buttoned up, and yet he had been shot through the heart. The dead man's pyjamas had been found in the locker of one of the students – wrapped in paper that smelled of garlic. And yesterday evening? Why had Münch, the lawyer, who had been visiting the Warden, kicked his friend Studer on the shin? Three times! Just because the sergeant had mentioned Frau Hungerlott's death.

Wottli ... Wottli ... Why could he not get that name out of his mind? Simply because it was written on the wrapping paper with the strange smell? He needed to find out if the cockerel really had poisoned itself. Not even that was certain, it sounded too much like an over-elaborate theory. Although one must never forget that reality was often more unbelievable than products of the imagination.

Perhaps Münch was following up a lead, perhaps he

was playing the private investigator because he was looking into a possible case of poisoning?

Suddenly the sergeant pulled a newspaper out of the inside pocket of his lined leather jacket. He wrapped the three handkerchiefs in one sheet and the dead bird in two others. He did have a struggle with Old Mother Trili, who refused to give up the body of her friend, but eventually Studer was clutching three packages in his arms. The way he made off with them looked almost like flight.

The three inmates stared after him as he left. When he reached the street that led to the Sun Inn, he looked around. Two dozen lads were standing along the boundary between the college and the poorhouse, with their mouths wide open, laughing, slapping their thighs and pointing with outstretched fingers at the running detective. A lean man, tall and clean-shaven, who was a little way away from the group (It must be Wottli! thought Studer), was unable to restrain their mockery. Again the sun broke through, shining on the façade of the college. At the far corner a window was open, and two heads could be made out. From there, too, came laughter, scornful laughter. The labourer from Amriswil and his stepbrother were mocking the fleeing detective.

"Just you lot wait," Studer muttered, "I'll show you." He turned the corner by the inn, dashed up the steps, went into the bar and dropped onto a chair. Huldi was behind the bar. The sergeant wiped his forehead, ordered a large beer and asked for a long piece of string. When she brought it, he tied up the three packages he had on the table. And as soon as that complicated operation was finished, he stood up and left the room. Huldi heard the roar as an engine started – Sergeant Studer was setting off for Bern.

In the capital

As the sergeant was driving through Burgdorf, it suddenly occurred to him that he had omitted to make the acquaintance of Wottli. And there was another thing he'd forgotten. He should have had a word with his friend Münch to find out what the lawyer from Bern could tell him about the murdered man's will and how much he had left. If the teacher from the college, Wottli, was to inherit something, then an unknown person had suddenly appeared in the case who was no less a suspect than, for example, his pupil, Ernst Äbi. The latter had concealed the dead Chinaman's bloodstained pyjamas in a locker that bore the number twenty-six . . . twenty-six – twice thirteen! Why that number? Studer shook his head, perhaps to clear it of the superstitious ideas connected with numbers, perhaps because the rain, which the wind was driving into his face, was stinging his cheeks and nose.

He knew that the body of James Farny had been taken to Forensic, so after the railway station he turned left. Dr Malapelle, whom he knew from previous cases, welcomed him effusively. He had not found much, he told the sergeant, on the body of the murdered man. Studer asked to see the body and was taken into a dazzlingly white room. The expression on the Chinaman's face seemed to be one of scorn, perhaps because his lips were no longer hidden by his moustache, so the corners of his mouth were visible, turned down towards his chin.

"I'll spare you the technical details, *Ispettore*. The bullet pierced his heart, the man was dead on the spot."

"Was there much blood?"

"*Sicuro!* There was no internal bleeding."

"From what distance did the shot come?"

"To estimate is *molto difficile* . . . very difficult. No scorch marks . . . probably twelve or fifteen feet."

"Calibre?"

"I guess 6.35."

"What?" Studer blinked in astonishment. "But that's a tiny bullet. Did you know, *Dottore*, that a large-calibre revolver, a Colt, almost a pocket machine-gun, was found beside the body? And that a shot had been fired from it?"

Dr Malapelle only called the sergeant "*Ispettore*" when he was pleased with him. When, however, he was annoyed with Studer, he changed to "*Sergente*", rolling the "r" as he pronounced the word.

"*No, Sergente,*" Malapelle said. Then he launched into the sergeant, telling him he was not a good detective, nor an intelligent one, for if he had been he would have seen from the bullet wound that it had been caused by a small-bore gun.

Studer scratched his neck, and the skin round his pointed nose wrinkled. He was embarrassed and furious with himself for not having examined the body more closely. But, after all, a simple detective sergeant is not expected to have the knowledge of a doctor; it was that Pfründisberg doctor with the beard that had not been trimmed for years who ought to have pointed out the discrepancy to him. Studer shrugged his shoulders and let his hands slap against his thighs.

But then he remembered the package he had tied to the pillion of his motorbike. He turned away from the dead body and dashed to the door, then paused and looked back at Dr Malapelle, telling him to wait for him upstairs in the laboratory. He'd brought a few things, he said, that looked as if they needed analysing.

"*Bene, bene, Ispettore,*" said the Dr Malapelle, once more content with the detective sergeant. He had a great liking for this policeman, whose massive build almost gave him the look of a clumsy peasant, because he spoke such excellent Italian. And not only that, he didn't ask boring questions; indeed, he was well informed on many scientific matters.

It was only a short time before Studer appeared in the laboratory on the second floor. He was panting because he'd taken the stairs two at a time.

"Here it is, *Dottore,*" he said. He placed the package on the table, took out an army knife and cut through the string.

"*Un gallo!*" Malapelle exclaimed, weighing the cockerel in his hand. "But why? What do you want me to do with it, *Ispettore?*"

"An autopsy," Studer commanded. "Then examine its intestines. I believe you'll find arsenic. Then I've got this" – he showed him the three handkerchiefs – "and this here" – he pointed to the brown wrapping paper with Wottli's name on it – "and, last of all, a pair of pyjamas."

Dr Malapelle's colourful tie was tied in a tiny knot between the points of his stiff collar. He fingered it as he examined all the objects in astonishment.

"Test them for arsenic? For 'As'?" he asked, using the chemical symbol for the element.

"Yes," said Studer with a nod, "for 'As'."

Quickly the Italian took off his jacket, slipped on a white laboratory coat and got down to work. Hansli, the feathered friend of a poorhouse woman, was opened up with a lancet, the contents of its crop deposited in a retort and covered with water. The flame of the Bunsen burner licked like a blue tongue at the wire gauze on which the globe of the retort stood, the water began to boil, the neck, with damp cloths wrapped round it, filled with steam. Now Dr Malapelle turned off the gas, the Bunsen burner withdrew its blue tongue, the damp cloths were taken away: the black arsenic mirror was clearly visible.

"Hmmmm," Studer muttered. "A poisoned cock, eh?"

Malapelle nodded. "*Senza dubbio* – no doubt about it."

Next it was the turn of the handkerchiefs. They, too, showed the presence of arsenic. Then came the wrapping paper – the arsenic mirror gleamed in the retort. Studer was confused. And his confusion was only increased when the last object, James Farny's pyjamas, was tested. The trousers had been in water for half an hour, and when the water in the retort was heated the neck remained clear. Drops of water formed on the inside, but no gleaming mirror. When the water, in which the pyjama jacket had been soaking for almost three-quarters of an hour, was heated, all that appeared was a transparent film, which hardly gleamed at all. Dr Malapelle said he presumed the brown paper the material was wrapped in was what had caused the weak reaction.

When Studer took out his watch, he realized he had taken up far too much of the poor man's time. He had arrived at the Institute for Forensic Medicine at half past eleven and now it was gone two o'clock. So the sergeant did the only sensible thing and invited the Italian to lunch. The motorbike roared across Bern. From time to time Dr Malapelle shouted pertinent remarks in Studer's ear from his seat on the pillion. But Frau Hedwig Studer was used to her husband's irregular mealtimes. The table was already set, and it took her no time at all to lay a third place.

The Italian stirred his soup with his spoon and kept on praising the aroma until Studer, in a tone of irritation, put an end to the compliments. He had not invited the *Dottore* to lunch, he said, to waste his time listening to idle flattery but to discuss . . .

The Italian cut him short. "I do not discuss when I am eating," he said.

Only when the black coffee had been served did he finally allow Studer to get a word in. The sergeant's wife, however, withdrew to the kitchen. She had some washing-up to do, she said, and anyway, she had no wish to hear about yet another murder. It was terrible being married to a detective, she went on, he was always late for meals, and when he did come he had nothing but deaths or thefts or robbery and murder on his mind.

"It was murder but not in the course of robbery this time," Studer said, still irritated, and began to recount the story of the Chinaman. He told Dr Malapelle about the dead body lying on a grave – the murderer obviously trying to make it look like suicide. But that was impossible, not only because the dead man's clothes were done up and undamaged, despite the shot to the heart, but also because, according to Dr Malapelle, the shot must have been fired from a distance of at least twelve feet.

"You remember that case in Gerzenstein, Malapelle, when we got to know each other? There it was the exact opposite. Suicide would have been a possibility because Witschi had stuffed the barrel of the pistol with cigarette papers to avoid any scorch marks. But eventually I established that someone else had shot the dead man from a distance of at least six feet, while everyone in the village assumed it was suicide. Even the examining magistrate who was dealing with the case still thinks so today. Apart from you and me, *Dottore*, there is only one woman who knows what really happened."

The Italian nodded. "The Witschi case."

"This one's even worse," said Studer. "There's not just the one name that ends in 'I', but three: Äbi, Wottli and Farny . . . Farny's what the dead man was called. Wottli teaches at a horticultural college, and his mother lives in Bern. She used the brown paper, which you showed had traces of arsenic, to send something to her son, probably his washing. Why was there arsenic on that paper, that brown wrapping paper? If you could answer me that question . . ."

"*Pazienza!*" Giuseppe Malapelle told him. Then he asked where the cock and the three handkerchiefs fitted in. Studer told him what had happened that morning.

"Perhaps you're barking up the wrong tree entirely, *Ispettore*," said the Italian. "You mustn't forget that all these things have happened in the vicinity of a horticultural college."

"What has a horticultural college to do with arsenic?"

"A great deal. In the first place a college like that will certainly have a chemistry course . . ."

"Aha!" said Studer, surprised. "That's right. Wottli teaches chemistry, amongst other things, the principal told me that this morning."

"There. You see? In the second place I am sure students at a college like that will be taught how to eradicate pests from plants. The pesticides that are used are all poisonous. Nicotine is used for lice, and pre-parations with arsenic to destroy caterpillars. Maybe the teacher – what did you say he was called? Wotschli? The names you have in Switzerland! What? Ah, Wottli. Good. – Maybe this Wottli opened the parcel some-where where the pesticides are kept, in the store per-haps. So the paper came into contact with such a substance and that was why we saw the arsenic mirror. Do you see that? Yes?"

Studer nodded. There was a lot to be said for the explanation; perhaps it was even the right one. The only thing against it was Frau Hungerlott's hand-kerchiefs. These had certainly not come into contact with a pesticide for caterpillars. So the sergeant rejected Dr Malapelle's argument. The Italian merely shrugged his shoulders.

"You must continue your search, *Ispettore*. You must go and see Wottli's mother and see if you can find the mother of Frau Hungerlott and Ernst Äbi, who was her brother, was he not?"

Studer nodded.

"Perhaps you will find out something important from both the mothers. Afterwards you must go back to Frundisbergo, for that is where you will find the solution – as you did in our first case together. There the answer was in the village. Forget 'As' for a while."

While Dr Malapelle said goodbye to Frau Studer in the hall, Studer stayed in his armchair. He had his hand over his eyes, but he wasn't asleep, he was think-ing. What was the significance of the kicks his friend Münch had given him?

Two mothers

Studer got up and went into the bedroom because that was where the telephone was, on the bedside table. He lifted the receiver and dialled the Post Office Giro Bank. He had to wait for a return call. After ten minutes his phone rang, and he was informed that James Farny had 6,325 Fr. deposited in his account. Quite a sum . . . From which bank had it been transferred? – Crédit Lyonnais.

Now Studer rang the Bern branch of the French bank. And they had a surprise in store for him. He had been afraid they would make difficulties, because of their duty of confidentiality towards their customers. But he found exactly the opposite. Farny had left instructions that enquiries about his account from the police were to be answered immediately. Just to make sure, they asked Herr Studer to ring off and they would call him back straight away. At his private number? Certainly . . . Then: the account contained $100,000 US and £10,000 sterling. Besides that, Herr Farny had rented a safe-deposit box, which contained precious stones. Diamonds, emeralds, rubies.

Carefully, respectfully, Studer replaced the receiver. He looked up the exchanges rates of foreign currency in the newspaper . . . The pound was standing at 15.03 and the dollar at 3.25. Quite a sum indeed! The Chinaman had left a fortune of a round half million Swiss francs. Not counting a safe-deposit box containing precious stones . . .

Studer felt something like nausea. Suddenly the case was getting on his nerves. What? It was all about an inheritance, nothing else? And once he'd found the lucky heir – or, rather, the lucky *heirs* – he would know who the murderer was? *Chabis!* He would still be nowhere near finding the guilty party. No, the case was getting less and less interesting. A man on a low income, a man who has not always had the best of luck during his life, never really enjoys securing a fortune for someone else. And anyway, who would pocket the Chinaman's fortune now?

The sergeant was sitting on the bed. The dreary day outside steeped the room in a dim half-light. Studer clenched his fist, raised it and stuck out his index finger: "Firstly, his sister . . ." he muttered. The middle finger shot up: "Secondly, her illegitimate son, the farm labourer . . ." Now it was the turn of his ring finger: "Thirdly, Ernst Äbi, the student at the horticultural college. Fourthly, his sister, Hungerlott's wife . . ." Studer stared at his hand. Only his thumb was left folded over. Now that shot up sideways, standing at a right angle to the palm: "And her husband? The warden of pauperism? Eh? And Äbi, the bricklayer . . . I've run out of fingers."

"Don't you want a coffee, Köbu?" came his wife's voice through the door.

"No!" the sergeant snapped angrily. He went over to the coat-stand, put on his jacket and overcoat and flung open the apartment door. But as he was about to slam it shut, he was overcome with remorse. He probably wouldn't be back until Sunday, he said in a quiet, friendly voice, it was one hell of a case. Frau Studer nodded sadly. On Sunday . . . and it was only Thursday. "Bye, Hedy." And Sergeant Studer shut the door carefully.

He mounted his motorbike and drove to 25 Aarbergergasse. He wanted to find out about Wottli, because the teacher had some wrapping paper that showed traces of arsenic.

The three-room apartment was on the first floor and was scrupulously clean. A woman who still looked young, despite her white hair (her face had no wrinkles), shuffled across the gleaming parquet floor in felt slippers. She started to talk as soon as she opened the door, and nothing could dam the flow of words. She spoke a strange Basel dialect spiced with Bernese expressions. It was presumably a long time since she'd left her hometown. She praised her son. How clever he was, and how astute . . . Ooh! He'd started in a market garden as a simple labourer, he'd never done an apprenticeship, since at the time his father had just died and there was no money in the house. Not a penny . . . He'd been sixteen when he'd started, had Paul, and he'd kept on changing his job so that he learned everything. First of all, a tree nursery, then vegetables, then roses and finally landscape gardening. Did the sergeant know what that was, landscaping? she asked. He didn't? Well, it was laying out new gardens. Ah yes, the plans Paul had made. Then he'd gone to Germany, near Berlin, to learn about perennials. They didn't have bedding plants any more, these new gardens, did they, it was all herb– . . . herbaceous: delphiniums and irises and phlox and asters and narcissuses or whatever the plants were called . . . After that, she went on, he'd gone to Stuttgart, the palm house of the royal palace, and had specialized in orchids . . .

"But do sit down, Sergeant. Do you want something to drink?"

Studer shook his head. He wanted to ask a question, he said, but that was all he got out, already the torrent of words had started up again. Yes, orchids! And in the evening he'd read books, until he'd learned enough to write articles, oh yes, scientific articles in periodicals, botanical journals!

The sergeant's head was ringing. There was nothing for it but to let the old woman with the fine white teeth carry on with her tale . . .

Then Paul had been brought back to Switzerland by a rich gentleman who had a castle by Lake Thun. Three workers he'd had under him, had Paul, and they'd had to look lively – Paul himself led by example, sometimes he'd worked fourteen hours a day. Then the rich gentleman had died, and to thank Paul for all his work he'd left him some money . . .

"How much?" Studer's question cut into the flow of words, but even that wasn't enough to stop it.

Five thousand francs! That was right, five thousand francs. A small fortune! And right away after that the government had appointed him to the horticultural college in Pfründisberg . . . Ooooh! And wasn't he popular with his students! Some of them, those on the one-year course, for example – but even the others, those who only took the winter course, even they never forgot Paul when they moved to a new position. That was how popular he was. He knew about everything, about composting, about pruning, the glasshouse . . . He was at home everywhere, was Paul . . .

"In chemistry as well?" Studer's second question was also sharp as a razor.

"Of course, of cooourse!" And the words continued to hail down on him like raindrops drumming on the windowpanes. Studer bowed his head. He was sitting in a red plush armchair, the armrests of which were certainly polished with wax every day. When Frau Wottli had finished the sergeant asked her, very gently, very carefully, what had been in the parcel she had sent to her son.

"Er, books." She'd sent Paul some books five days ago. Why did he want to know that?

"Just asking . . ." Had Paul been friendly with a man called Farny who had had a room at the Sun Inn in Pfründisberg?

Farny? Of course he had! At one time Herr Farny – presumably the sergeant meant the Herr Farny who had been found dead yesterday morning? – Well, at one time this Herr Farny had intended to build a house – in Pfründisberg – and he'd asked her son whether he'd like to draw up a plan for the garden. The plans her Paul could draw up! Marvellous! Even the head of the city gardens was sometimes astonished at what Paul could do, and he'd asked him to come to Bern during the college vacation to assist him in planting out the botanical garden . . . Oh yes, it was . . . But she was sure Herr Studer must be very thirsty by now, what would he like to drink? She had a particularly good strawberry schnapps, made with a new variety Paul had cultivated in Pfründisberg. Wouldn't the sergeant like to try it?

The sergeant nodded, thanked her and said he would be driving back to Pfründisberg that evening.

Frau Wottli went into the kitchen, came back with a bottle, filled two glasses and clinked glasses with the sergeant.

Just as Studer was putting his glass back down on the little round table a racket started up somewhere in the building. Chairs fell over, plates shattered as they crashed to the floor; it all sounded as if there were a hailstorm in the house. The idea of a summer thunderstorm was suggested by the fact that the noise definitely came from the second floor.

"Who lives up there?" Studer asked, pointing to the ceiling.

Now a woman's voice cried out, loud and plaintive.

Frau Wottli shook her head. Äbi had come home early today, she said. And no doubt he'd been drinking again. Now he was beating his wife . . .

"Äbi?" the sergeant asked. "Have they any children?"

"Yes. A son and a daughter." The daughter had made an excellent marriage, Frau Wottli said, her husband was high up, but what good had it done poor Anna? None whatsoever! She'd died not long ago. The son wasn't up to much. He'd done nothing with his life, just worked as a labourer. Only now, when he was nearly thirty, had he managed to get into Pfründisberg, and that just because a rich uncle from abroad had helped him . . .

"And their father?"

A month ago the Welfare had found him a temporary job with a coal merchant. He earned one franc an hour . . .

"Not much," said Studer.

No, it wasn't, she agreed, but he was often absent, was Arnold Äbi, and not only on a Monday. He'd have stopped work at three again today to go drinking. "Oh yes, the man's quite different from my Paul. *My* son doesn't drink."

Studer looked at the old woman closely. To the right of her nose was a mole that bobbed up and down, like a brown fisherman's float on a stream. In his mind's eye the image of Wottli, the teacher, came into clearer and clearer focus, and the fact that the man was a "scientist" added the final touch. The sergeant had come across many men who had acquired their knowledge from books – mostly autodidacts who got it from the encyclopaedia. Such men usually went round with the conviction, like an invisible helmet, that they knew about anything and everything. But their every idea was wrong. They thought themselves omniscient, but often, all too often, their pride sent them down the wrong path. They were rarely happy ... Was Wottli one of those? Once he'd inherited five thousand francs – was he hoping for a larger sum this time? The sergeant sighed. He was a peaceable fellow and didn't like stirring up pointless arguments. But such arguments were what lay in store for him, they would crop up at his first interview with the teacher at the college. Upstairs the woman's crying grew louder, slaps could be heard.

So Jakob Studer took his leave. But he still did not manage to make the acquaintance of Arnold Äbi. As he came out of Frau Wottli's apartment he heard the downstairs door slam shut and moaning from the floor above. He crept up the stairs quietly; he had no need to fear Frau Wottli would hear him, she had gone back to her living room. A woman was lying on the landing outside the open door. Her short, greasy, grey hair stuck out in a tousled mop; she was wearing a black cotton dress with a blue apron. The heels of her brown shoes were drumming on the red tiles. Above the grubby doorbell a visiting card had been fixed with a drawing pin to the doorframe:

Arnold Äbi
Master Bricklayer

Studer bent down, put his arms under the quivering body, straightened up and went into the apartment. A corridor – no carpet on the dusty wooden floor – a room, clean, with not much furniture. There was a brown blanket thrown over the double bed, and he laid the woman down on it. She groaned softly. She was at least sixty, with a high forehead. Between her half-closed lids the white gleam of the cornea showed. Her lips parted, revealing two teeth that were broad and long and yellow, like a horse's teeth. First of all a groan: "Ah-ooo-aah!" Then her eyelids opened fully; the iris was a dull brown, like the blanket she was lying on. "Water," the woman groaned. Studer went out into the corridor, closing the door to the room behind him, then went into the kitchen. Pieces of broken plates were scattered over the floor, a chair was lying against the wall, its two front legs broken, the table was covered with scraps of paper, dirty forks and spoons. A vice was fixed to the edge. Studer touched it – filings stuck to his fingers.

A vice . . . iron filings . . . What had been filed down here?

The sergeant rinsed out a glass, filled it and went back into the room. The woman stretched out her hand, drank the water and fell back onto the bed.

"Who are you?" she asked. Studer told her his name.

"What do you want?"

"Nothing special . . ."

The woman swallowed, and her Adam's apple rolled up and down like a marble under a loose piece of cloth. It was slowly starting to get dark in the room; suddenly the lamps went on out in the street, sticking yellow rectangles of light to the ceiling. The woman remained silent; her face was in the dark. Her dress had long tears revealing a patterned cotton petticoat underneath.

"Why did he hit you?" Studer asked.

A sigh. The nails of her left hand were scratching at the blanket, otherwise there was no sound to be heard, the road outside was quiet. Then the woman answered with a question: "What business is it of yours if my husband hits me?" She gave a short, shrill laugh.

"Don't your children help their mother?" the sergeant asked. The word "mother" brought the prostrate woman to life. She sat up and put her feet on the floor. She did stagger a little as she pushed off from the edge of the bed, but then she walked steadily across the room. There was the soft snap of a switch, then dazzling brightness, even though the bulb had blue crepe paper wrapped round it

"My children!" the woman said, digging her fingers into her short-cropped hair. "My children!" she repeated. "I had a daughter, but she died. I had two sons, but one's disappeared and the other doesn't want to know his mother because he hates his father . . . Yes, yes . . ." She sighed. "He doesn't want to know his Mamma, he prefers to go and see his other mother, who lives in the same building. Down there . . ." She pointed at the floor. "He spends hours sitting there, but he only stays here for five minutes."

"You mean Ernst?" Studer asked.

"Ernst? Is that what he was called?" A smile made her mouth seem even bigger, and her two front teeth dug into her lower lip. "Yes, one was called Ernst and the other Ludwig. The one Ernst Äbi, Ludwig Farny the other. I heard that both of them were in Pfründisberg. One at the horticultural college and the other in the poorhouse. Is that true, Herr . . . Herr . . .?"

"Studer."

"Oh, right . . . Is that true, Herr Studer? Or is Ludwig still in Thurgau?"

The sergeant wondered whether the woman was putting on an act, or whether she was really ill. Perhaps she had a fever, she certainly didn't look well. Her face was thin, and there were shiny patches of red on her cheekbones. She started coughing, went over to the bedside table, panting and wheezing, opened a drawer and began to rummage round among the things inside. Suddenly she cried out.

"What's wrong?" Studer asked.

"Nothing . . . oh . . . nothing." She had gone pale, the only colour left in her face was the tiny spots of red on her cheekbones.

"Perhaps . . . I . . . I don't know. The doctor prescribed some medicine for me and it's gone. Perhaps Noldi took them. But what would he want them for?"

It sounded strange. How could the woman use such a tender, familiar name for the husband who had beaten her up so badly? He was called Arnold, and she still called him Noldi.

"What was it?"

"A sedative," the woman said. "Tablets . . . White tablets . . . Or perhaps Frau Wottli's taken them? I gave her one once, a week ago, and it helped. She managed to get to sleep after she'd taken it. And she came to see me this morning. Perhaps . . ."

Studer took out his watch. Six o'clock! He'd have to hurry if he wanted to get back to Pfründisberg that evening. So he said goodbye to the sick woman, promising to come again soon, and he asked whether he should send Frau Wottli up. "So that you won't be all alone if you feel ill. Perhaps," he added in questioning tones, "I should go to a chemist's and get some of the tablets your doctor prescribed. Have you still got the prescription?"

The woman shook her head, telling him it wasn't possible. The chemist had kept the prescription. It was a narcotic.

A narcotic? Studer let out a soft whistle. Pity he didn't know what it was the doctor had prescribed the

89

woman. It was too late by now to go and call on the doctor. He could always go to police headquarters and set the necessary steps in motion, but Studer couldn't be bothered. When a case was still all in a tangle, he preferred not to bring in colleagues. That was all right once he'd got hold of the end of the thread. But it wasn't worth making a fuss just for some narcotic pills that had gone missing. There was such a mess in the Äbi apartment, the old woman could simply have mislaid them. He had a quick look in the open drawer and saw there were lots of packs and tubes and phials: tonics and sleeping pills and drugs for the heart. He picked up the biggest bottle. It was empty. He looked at the labels. "Poison" it said on one of them; another, above it, had a skull and two crossed bones. Then, on the largest, he read "Fowler's Solution". Yet another arsenic preparation!

"Who emptied this bottle?" Studer asked.

"I did," said the woman. Again her fingers were burrowing into her short-cropped white hair.

When Studer came to the first-floor landing, he stopped for a moment outside Frau Wottli's door. He listened. A bell rang inside; there was a click as the telephone was picked up.

"Oh . . . yes . . . Hello, Paul . . . Yes, he's been to see me. This afternoon . . . He left a long time ago, he'll soon be there . . . No, no . . . No! I haven't been up to see Frau Äbi. Should I go . . .? The living-room door's open, I'll go and close it . . . Yes, I'm going now."

Studer heard steps coming closer. He didn't move.

Inside the apartment a door was closed.

Studer left the building.

A round of *Jass* with a new partner

The fog was thick. A lamp was burning over the door to the inn, casting a little light on the steps leading up to it from the road. And a man was waiting at the foot of the stone flight.

As soon as Studer had switched off the engine he heard his name called.

"Yes?" he growled.

"Paul Wottli. I'm a teacher at Pfründisberg Horticultural College."

Studer took off his woollen glove, only to feel a spurt of irritation when the man who had just introduced himself did not shake his hand but just held out three fingers, keeping his elbow pressed to his side.

"I've been waiting for you all afternoon, Herr Studer," the man said. "All afternoon! How can you simply drop an investigation in order to go to Bern? I thought that solving a murder was a serious matter. I'm very well read, you know, including that area."

It was a cold November evening, and Studer was freezing, despite his long johns and his woollen pullover. He was not in the best of moods and looking forward to a hot supper, but still he had to laugh at Wottli's little speech.

"And what interesting books have made you an expert criminologist, Herr Wottli?" he asked.

"Well, I've read Gross, I've read Locard in French, I subscribe to the *Criminal Archives* . . ."

"Yes, thank you, Herr Wottli, you've convinced me.

In that case, you will understand that I needed to go to the city to make certain enquiries."

"Enquiries! Enquiries! They are of no use whatsoever, Herr Studer, if one has not first subjected the premises already found to logical analysis. You understand? I find it absolutely erroneous to place one of my students under the supervision of an incriminating youth from the poorhouse and then to lock the pair of them up in the sickbay. I therefore took the liberty of releasing Ernst Äbi, since I required him for an important task this evening. It was necessary to fill the glasshouse with hydrogen cyanide gas this evening in order to kill off the pests that regale themselves on my orchids and the leaves of my palms. That was why I went to fetch my student at half past five – I would willingly have asked your permission first, but it was urgent, so I acted on my own authority. I felt, however, that it was necessary to inform you of my decision in order to forestall any mistaken suspicion that might arise. You understand?"

Studer nodded reflectively. Strange, the way everything fitted . . . Premises, incriminating – the misuse of certain words.

"I would very much like to have my dinner, Herr Wottli," Studer said, also using High German. "May I invite you to a coffee? After you . . ."

They went up the steps. The innkeeper was waiting for them at the door and asked what the sergeant would like to eat. Then he opened the door to the private room, the one with the oven coated with aluminium paint – it was lit and filled the room with a cosy warmth. Hulda Nüesch brought a hot toddy, then the sergeant's supper, and for Herr Wottli a black concoction in a tall glass.

The sergeant took his time over his meal and tried to

forget the case for a while, despite Wottli's chatter. Four men came in, said "Good evening" and sat down at a table by the window: Sack-Amherd, Hungerlott, Schranz, the farmer, and a man Studer did not know with a long, shiny red nose that looked like a caricature.

"Good evening, Herr Äbi." The teacher stood up, held out two fingers to the man with the red nose, then resumed his seat opposite the sergeant.

"The father of one of my students," he whispered but in a loud enough voice for everyone in the room to hear. Studer muttered something incomprehensible.

So that was the man who called himself a "master bricklayer" on his visiting card, beat his wife and drank too much. How had he managed to get to Pfründisberg so quickly? He'd slammed shut the door of the house in Aarbergergasse at a quarter past five, and here he was already. When had he got to Pfründisberg? It was Hungerlott who supplied the explanation. As he took out a pack of cards and started to shuffle them, he launched into a long story, pointing to the man on his left. He'd been in town that afternoon, he said, he'd had things to do, orders to place because he was expecting visitors on Saturday – commissions for a Commission, heheheh, because that's what was coming at the weekend. Representatives of the Health Board, members of the Canton parliament – and two junior doctors from some care-home were coming to Pfründisberg to find out what was being done to combat "pauperism" ... Yes ... So he'd taken the car to Bern that day – and who did they think he'd run into outside the station at a quarter to six? Herr Äbi! There had a been a time, years ago now, of course, when there'd been talk of putting Äbi away in Pfründisberg – heheheh. But after the warden had become the said Äbi's son-in-law no one had suggested he be added to the list of the poorhouse inmates ... Hungerlott glanced at the sergeant out of the corner of his eye, Sack-Amherd rolled up the sleeves of his purple shirt, then picked up and looked at the cards he had been dealt. Äbi grunted, the cards in his hand were quivering; finally he looked up and croaked – his voice was hoarse – "Your call," to which Schranz replied "Spades."

There was a clock on the wall between the two windows, through which the green shimmer of the wooden shutters could be seen. It struck three times, sounding as if its bell was cracked. Studer looked up at it: a quarter to ten. The four went on with their game of *Jass*, Hungerlott and Sack-Amherd playing quickly and confidently, Äbi and the farmer slowly and hesitantly. From time to time a mild argument broke out because Äbi spent too long thinking.

Studer asked Wottli, "It was at six that you started the fumigation, wasn't it? When did you finish?"

"Is it important? Or are you just testing me? If that's what you're doing, I can give you a precise reply. It was completed at a quarter past six, and I locked the door from the glasshouse to the corridor. At a quarter past six – or eighteen-fifteen, if you prefer."

Studer nodded and nodded. He drew on his Brissago and cast a vague glance at the evening paper he'd bought in Bern.

Schranz stood up. He had to pop back to his farm, he said, one of his cows was due to calve that night, did the sergeant fancy taking his place for a while – for fifteen minutes, it wouldn't be more?

Studer nodded his agreement and sat down opposite the red-nosed Äbi. It was Hungerlott's deal and Äbi's turn to declare trumps or pass. He found it difficult to decide. He fanned out his cards slowly, sticking them in an untidy row between his thumb and his crooked forefinger. He swore, scratched his head and moaned that he didn't know what to do until eventually Studer barked at him to get on with it and make up his mind. The little eyes – they were dull, like his wife's – shot him a venomous glance, and he wailed, "I'm passing." – "Clubs," said Studer. He had the king and queen, the ten and the three lowest trumps as well as the ace of spades and two low hearts.

His partner led. Studer was puzzled that instead of playing trumps he threw the ten of hearts on the cloth. Sack-Amherd played the ace, Studer trumped with the king and Hungerlott took the trick with the ace of trumps. It turned into a disaster. The laughter of the two winners was so loud, the innkeeper peered round the door, Wottli made jokes, and the losers swore, softly but with conviction.

Although Studer always insisted he only played *Jass* for what one might call psychological reasons, in order to learn about the character of those he played with, he still got annoyed – that evening especially – when he lost. Now it was the turn of the former bricklayer to deal (wasn't he working for a coal merchant now and kept taking days off?), and even the way he dealt the cards was irritating. He licked his thumb and stuck it on the top card before he dealt the card, then licked his fingers again, for the next card, and so on until he'd finished dealing. Hungerlott said he had ten cards and they had to be dealt again. Finally they all had the right number, and Sack-Amherd chose trumps. All at once Studer's irritation vanished. He fixed his gaze on his partner and slowed the game down.

Äbi was trembling! Of course, it might be the alcohol that was causing it. But still! But still! There was something else. The whole time the man seemed to be waiting for something. He had large, red ears, flat at

the top and they stood out from his head. His ears told
Studer that Äbi was listening intently. Now he would
turn his head towards the door out into the corridor,
now towards the door to the adjoining room. And
when he did so, he closed his eyes. That proved that it
was a noise he was expecting. What kind of noise?

Studer decided to stir things up a little. After he had
counted the tricks they had won, he snapped at his
partner, "Can't you play better than that?" He could
play as well as any cop, was the answer he got.

"Now then, now then," said Hungerlott in placatory
tones. Then he turned to the sergeant, explaining that
he had invited his father-in-law to stay the night. There
was enough room, he said, since his wife had died. Äbi
could sleep in the same room; there were two beds
in it.

Studer cleared his throat and looked from one to
the other before fixing his gaze on the teacher who was
so well read in criminology. Wottli had placed his hands
on Äbi's shoulders. The nails of his long, thin fingers
were digging into the cloth of the grubby jacket.

Then, suddenly, the sergeant felt as if the events
of 18 July were being repeated. Noise came from the
next room, the sound of glasses being broken. Then
the five men heard the innkeeper calling for help.
Studer pushed his chair back, leaped to the door and
tore it open.

The innkeeper was surrounded by four men in
greasy blue overalls – two were holding his arms – and
in the corner Huldi was trying to ward off three other
men from the poorhouse. The sergeant recognized
those three; that morning they had been shuffling
round the yard with brooms.

Studer stepped in quickly. He liberated the innkeeper by grasping the two who were holding him

round the back of their necks and knocking their heads together. At that the two others dashed off. He meted out the same treatment to two of those who were holding Huldi, but a third, who had been pulling her hair, drew back his fist. He tried to punch Studer, but the sergeant ducked, and the fist went through a windowpane. The other four made off, rubbing their sore heads, the last following them after he had wrapped a handkerchief round his bleeding hand. Silence. Two figures stood in the doorway to Brönnimann's private room: Sack-Amherd swinging his watch chain, Hungerlott playing with his widower's ring.

"Where are the others?"

"They've just left, Sergeant. Wottli said he would go and see that everything was all right at the college."

"Hmmmm . . ." Studer was pinching his nose with his thumb and forefinger and seemed to be listening. Through the broken window he could hear a strange noise, it sounded like the muttering of a crowd of people. When he opened the window he saw there was a gathering below. About thirty upturned faces were illuminated by the light from the room. And the sergeant immediately recognized them; they had been grinning at him that morning when he fled from the courtyard of the poorhouse. All the students from the horticultural college seemed to be there, staring up at the window.

Why did the sergeant have the feeling it was all a put-up job? Or, to be more precise, a well-rehearsed play? The men from the poorhouse had no reason to attack the innkeeper and the waitress. It looked as if the purpose of the racket had been to attract the students from the college. What else could Arnold Äbi, the father-in-law of the warden, have been waiting for? Was that why he had been listening? And why had he immediately left the room, accompanied by Wottli? There was another thing that struck the sergeant, as he silently leaned on the window ledge: the ground floor of the college was brightly lit and to the right of the main building, about fifty yards away, a cube, a glass cube appeared to be glowing. The glasshouse . . .

Apprehensively, Studer scanned the windows of the façade; those on the first floor were closed and dark. But if he looked closely, he could see the individual panes, for they reflected tiny specks of light. The last window, however, was open, and there was something white dangling down from the window ledge to the ground, swaying to and fro in the wind. The wind that had subsided at midday had risen again and dispersed the fog.

Studer looked down at the students again, to see if he could find Ernst Äbi, whom he had placed under the supervision of a former inmate of the poorhouse, but he could not see his suspect. Suddenly, however, a figure started to push its way with difficulty through the crowd.

"Sergeant!" shouted Ludwig Farny. "Sergeant Studer! Quick, quick! My brother's lying on the floor in the glasshouse."

A chain of thought rapidly formed in the sergeant's mind: glasshouse – fumigation – hydrogen cyanide . . . He shouted to Ludwig to come up, then he closed the window. In one corner Huldi was sitting, her pale skin even paler than usual. Haltingly, she asked if something had happened to Ludwig.

"No," Studer growled, "your boyfriend's just coming."

Ludwig. Always Ludwig. The door to the neighbouring room was closed. The door to the corridor opened, and Ludwig came in.

In the glasshouse

"It's not my fault, Herr Studer! It was Ernst, he gave me the slip. I know I should have kept watch, but I was so tired, Herr Studer, so tired. I've been concentrating all day, I wanted you to be pleased with me. But I fell asleep, Herr Studer, after Herr Wottli locked us in again. Ernst went to bed too and snored like anything. Now I know he was just pretending, but at the time I thought he was really asleep. *Really*. God knows, it wasn't my fault."

The sergeant sat down astride a chair, rested his forearms on the back and said nothing. If confusion reigned, then he was going to think everything through calmly first of all and then decide what was to be done. Paul Wottli had begun the fumigation at six; at six-fifteen he'd finished. Then he'd taken the two lads – why was it he'd only talked about Ernst and not mentioned Ludwig? – anyway, he'd taken the two lads back to the sickbay and locked them in. Yes, but he'd told Studer he'd gone to fetch Ernst at half past five. Even assuming the preparations for the fumigation took a quarter of an hour, that still left a quarter of an hour unaccounted for. Hungerlott claimed he'd met his father-in-law at a quarter to six at the railway station, so the earliest he could have arrived, if he'd driven fast, would have been at five past six. Since, however, it had been foggy, he would certainly have taken longer and probably not reached Pfründisberg until around half past six. Studer recalled that the station clock had said ten to seven when he had driven past and that it had been a quarter to nine when he had finished his dinner. So he had taken at least fifty minutes on his motorbike to get from Bern to Pfründisberg. Ten minutes for his conversation with Wottli outside the inn; thirty minutes to eat his dinner; fifteen minutes for his cigar and the evening paper. So he must have arrived between half past seven and a quarter to eight . . .

"Sit yourself down, Ludwig," he said and, turning to the waitress, "Huldi, bring him a beer."

And Studer waited until the lad had finished his beer before telling him to wipe his brow. "You rushed over as fast as you could?"

"Yes, I did." Ludwig nodded a few times. He said he'd thought it was urgent.

Studer shrugged his powerful shoulders. Urgent! Once someone was in a place filled with hydrogen cyanide gas, getting him out wasn't urgent. Three minutes, that was enough. After that any attempt to rescue him would be in vain.

"Now tell me exactly what happened. It was not necessary to hurry." Ludwig Farny opened his blue eyes wide in astonishment and stared at the broad-shouldered sergeant. It was the first time he had heard him speak formal German. He tried to follow suit.

"I heard this racket," he said, paused then corrected himself, "I heard a loud noise and that woke me up. It was dark in the room. Old Wott . . . Herr Wottli had locked us in at half past six. I'd gone with them before, when they went to fumigate the glasshouse. You told me to keep an eye on my brother, didn't you, Herr Studer?"

Ludwig Farny paused. He was still out of breath and wide-eyed. Then he went on:

"It was a quarter after six when they'd finished, and

the teacher turned the key in the lock. There was a lamp on inside, and I looked in through the glass. There's panes in the top half of the door, you know, and you can see inside the glasshouse, a tray with orchids on the left, tall palms in the middle and small larkspur – *delphinium chinese* the teacher called them, he said he grew them for special occasions.

"On the way back to the school building Herr Wottli asked us lots of questions. He wanted to know what you'd found in Ernst's locker, but my brother held his tongue. He said nothing, he kept looking this way and that, as if he was waiting for something. I asked him if he was looking for someone, but he just shook his head. Then we were in the sickbay, listening to the teacher going away. The only odd thing was that he didn't lock the door. Ernst went to the window and looked out. Suddenly he said he had to go and just get something from his desk. And he went. I was going to go with him, but he asked me not to. He was away half an hour and he came back empty-handed. He was hardly back in the room when Wottli opened the door and said, 'If you're going to be walking round the building by yourself, I'll have to lock you in. I will, of course, report your absence.' Ernst shrugged his shoulders, and we heard the key turn in the lock. Ernst got undressed and went to bed. Me too. Then my brother put the light out and I fell asleep straight away."

"What?" asked Studer in astonishment. "You went to sleep at seven o'clock?"

"I think it was later. I can't say exactly when it was because there's one thing I forgot. The teacher came back with some dinner for us: roast sweet corn, stewed prunes and coffee. Yes, that was it. We ate and then we went to bed."

Why . . . Why were the warden and the principal of the college still in the next room? The door was still closed.

"Go on," Studer growled. "And don't keep forgetting half of it."

"Yes, of course. Suddenly I heard a noise and I woke up with a start. I got out of bed and switched the light on. Then I realized I was alone – and the window was open. I leaned out. There was something white hanging down from the lower hinge of the green shutter. Ernst had tied two sheets together. They reached the ground, and he'd climbed out of the window. So I thought, if he can do it, so can I. I got dressed and climbed down. Then I ran over to the glasshouse because I could see that the light was still on, and I remembered clearly that the teacher had switched off the light when we left earlier. I went into the vestibule – there was a light burning there and in the section we'd fumigated. Ernst was in there, lying on the floor, his head was on his arms and his legs all twisted . . . I dashed out and ran and ran to fetch you, Herr Studer. You see, I'd noticed something: I tried to open the door to help Ernst, but it was locked – and the key was in the lock on the inside. I can swear to that. I thought Ernst had committed suicide. What do *you* think? Is that what he did? He knew the glasshouse was full of hydrogen cyanide and he knew it would be fatal to go in."

Silence. Studer sat astride his chair, his chin on his forearms, which were crossed and resting on the back.

"So . . ." He raised his head and nodded, nodded. "So Ernstli's dead." He felt partly to blame for the lad's death. He remembered his face with a nose sticking out that was so long it looked like a caricature. Had the lad killed himself because a detective had searched his locker and found a pair of bloodstained pyjamas?

"Go and fetch the principal, Ludwig," Studer said wearily, jerking his thumb at the door to the neighbouring room. The young man knocked shyly.

"Come in."

"You're to come and see Herr Studer." A muttering was to be heard, a chair being pushed back, then steps and a voice asking, "What do you want, Sergeant?"

"You'll have to come to the glasshouse with me."

"Has there been an accident?"

"Yes. Ernst Äbi's dead. He's in the glasshouse. Have you got a thin pair of pliers?"

"Pliers?" Herr Sack-Amherd repeated. "I think there's a pair in the toolkit in the corridor outside the . . . outside the departments that . . ."

"Let's go," Studer sighed and stood up. It felt as if he had a heavy weight resting on his shoulders and he was cold. Shivers ran down his back like icy water. But he pulled himself together.

"You're coming with us, Ludwig," he commanded and went out into the corridor. As he stopped to wait for the others he heard Huldi tell Ludwig to be careful and make sure nothing happened to him. Ludwig did not reply.

At the bottom of the steps Studer paused again. "Where's Hungerlott?" he asked.

"He wished me good night and went home by the terrace. He said he wasn't interested in all that. He had more important things to do. His friend, Münch, was waiting for him. He told me he'd arranged a meeting with him. About Farny's will . . ."

Sack-Amherd sighed. It sounded like a sigh of envy. Presumably the principal of the horticultural college begrudged his friend Hungerlott his good fortune in coming into an inheritance that would make him rich. Studer wondered whether he had interpreted the sigh correctly, so as they set off he asked, "Do you know any details of the will?"

Sack-Amherd sucked in the night air and breathed out stertorously, then told Studer that after the death of Frau Hungerlott, James Farny had changed his will and named the warden as heir.

"Did he now?" said Studer, drawing out the words.

There was the glasshouse. Three steps led up to a corridor, the left-hand side of which was taken up by a long table with a cement top that was let into the wall.

On it were three heaps: sand, peat and fine compost. Studer began to play with them, peat in his left hand, sand in his right. Then he opened his fingers. Gradually his hands felt lighter; it was a strange sensation to feel the weight disappear. And when would he be freed of that other burden, the guilt that weighed on him? Had it really been a mistake to absent himself from Pfründisberg that afternoon?

Studer turned away from the table and brushed his hands clean.

"Where is he?" he asked, for he could see two doors. Silently, Ludwig pointed to one. The upper part was of glass while the bottom consisted of tin that was painted green. Studer went up to it and stared for a long time through the panes, which were slightly misted, then took out his handkerchief to clear them, but the tiny drops were on the inside. That was why the body lying on the floor looked so strangely distorted. The sergeant bent down. He could see the key sticking out of the lock on the inside; it was blackened and covered in little red spots of rust. Studer turned round and asked Sack-Amherd:

"I suppose we can't go in? It'd be too dangerous, wouldn't it? Can it be ventilated?

Oh, yes, it could be ventilated, said the principal, pointing to a handle. With the crank it was possible to open the skylights in the roof, thus creating a draught.

Since the principal showed no desire to carry out the task, the sergeant told Ludwig to do it.

The crank screeched, an eerie sound in the silence.

"Now we must wait five minutes," said Sack-Amherd.

Studer went back to the cement table and played with the compost and peat, like a little boy in a sandpit. He smoothed out the heaps, drew runes on them, crosses, circles, zigzags – until a voice called from the door:

"Who opened those windows? What about my orchids? And my palms?"

Without looking up from his childish amusement, Studer said very quietly:

"There's a dead man in there, Herr Wottli."

"A dead man? What dead man? No one could get into the glasshouse, I've still got the key in my pocket."

"Have you?" the sergeant said wearily. "You carry the key in your pocket? May I see it?"

"There you are."

The key Studer had in his hand was exactly like the one in the lock: it too was blackened and had a few tiny specks of rust.

"*Meerci*," said Studer in his broadest Swiss accent, slipping the key into his trouser pocket. "Have you got a key, Principal?"

"Me? No."

"Where have you been just now, Herr Wottli?"

"Is that of interest to you, Sergeant? Well first of all, I accompanied the father of . . . of . . . the dead man to the poorhouse. Neither of us knew Ernst Äbi was dead. How could we?"

Studer lowered his head, dropping his chin onto his chest, and peered up at the teacher. Could he be mistaken? It seemed to him that Wottli was cowed, more even: apprehensive. As if the man was trying to hide something . . .

"And then?"

"Then I came back and got the students, who were standing outside the inn, to return to the main building. They had no business down there. But that was all I could do. They absolutely refused to go to bed. They're all downstairs in the classroom now, taking part in endless discussions. I stayed with them for a while, but then I looked out of the window and saw that there was a light on in the glasshouse, so I came over to see what was going on. I remembered – quite clearly remembered – that I had put the light out."

"And none of the students told you there was a dead body in the glasshouse? That's odd. They all heard Ludwig when he shouted up to me with the news."

Wottli was not so easy to catch out. Ah, he said, now he understood. Now he understood why they all wanted to take the path past the glasshouse when they came back. "But I didn't want them to do that because I knew it was dangerous, being filled with hydrogen cyanide gas. That's why I took one of the paths . . ."

"One of the paths from which you couldn't see that there was a light on in the glasshouse?"

"It was foggy . . ."

"No!" Studer spoke sharply. "No, the wind dispersed the fog ages ago." Then he smiled, raised his head, gave the teacher a long look and said, "You should read what old Gross has to say about witness statements."

Five minutes is a long time when you have to wait, but this time it had passed quickly. Studer found the toolkit, but the small pliers were missing. Strange. But he still managed to push the key out of the lock; it fell to the ground inside the glasshouse. The sergeant took Herr Wottli's key, opened the door and went in.

Ernst Äbi was lying on the floor, his shoulders convulsed. The sergeant went down on one knee, turned the body over and felt under his waistcoat – there was no heartbeat. To be absolutely sure, he held a round mirror to Ernst's lips – the glass did not mist over.

Only then did he start to search through the dead man's pockets. In the jacket pocket he found a catapult such as boys use to shoot at birds. The sergeant slipped the toy into his pocket. In the inside pocket was a wallet, filled with documents; that too, the sergeant pocketed. In the right trouser pocket: a purse. Contents: a twenty-franc note, a five-franc note, coins. In the left pocket: a box with white pills. Studer stood up. He sniffed at the pills, picked one out, licked it with the tip of his tongue . . . It tasted bitter. He held the box out to Sack-Amherd. "Do you recognize this?" he asked. The principal shook his head. But then Wottli broke in. The Herr Direktor must remember, he said, it was Uspulun, the new disinfectant for cyclamen seeds the German chemical firm had sent for testing. Three weeks ago. Ernst Äbi had been given the task of carrying out the tests – what concentration was best, how long the seeds should stay in the liquid. The . . . the dead man had drawn up a table, it was sure to be in his desk . . .

And what, Studer wanted to know, did Herr Wottli think the disinfectant contained?

"Arsenic, it's an organic arsenic compound . . ."

"Is it indeed?" Studer nodded. "Arsenic! Are you quite sure?"

"Quite sure, Sergeant."

Silence again. The buzzing of a winter fly could

clearly be heard. Once more Studer kneeled down, placed his forefinger and ring finger on the dead man's lids and closed Ernst's eyes.

He stood up, brushed the dust from his trousers – and then he heard a voice behind him:

"It can't be! My son! My son!"

Studer turned around abruptly. In the door was his *Jass* partner, his long nose glowing red . . .

"What are you doing here?" the sergeant snapped.

"It's my son! It's my son!" The man had taken his handkerchief out and was rubbing his eyes, blowing his nose.

"Stop making a scene," said Studer curtly, for the man's eyes were dry, even the blowing of his nose was not really convincing. "Who let him in?"

"I followed all the rest," said Arnold Äbi in a tearful voice, "and I don't know how I'm going to break the sad news to my wife . . ."

"If you don't feel up to it" – Studer still sounded impatient – "I'd be happy to ring Bern and get an officer from the City Police to go to Aarbergergasse and break it gently to Ernst's mother. But perhaps Ludwig would like to do it? Eh? When did you last go to see your mother?"

Ludwig, his eyes brimming with tears, shook his head. "First my uncle," he said in a strained voice, 'then my brother. Will it be my mother next?"

"Don't say such stupid things." growled Äbi. Studer turned his head in surprise. When had the man crept over there? Only seconds ago he had been in the vestibule, now he was by the dead man's head.

"What are you doing there?"

"Doing? Nothing." Again Arnold Äbi shot him a venomous glance, then he headed for the steps; he walked silently because he was wearing rubber soles.

Studer returned to the section where the dead body was lying – and there was a surprise in store for him. He went to pick up the key he'd pushed out of the lock, bent down . . . Instead of the blackened key with the flecks of rust, he found a new one on the floor, bright and shiny. He checked the door. The old key Wottli had given him was still in the lock on the outside.

Studer weighed the shiny key in his hand, making it gleam in the lamplight, then grasped it between thumb and forefinger and waggled it. Why had the rusty key been replaced with this one? Why? The answer was easy if one assumed it was not suicide but murder. But if it really was murder, it was difficult to see how it had been carried out. Ernst Äbi must have been forced to leave the sickbay; the two sheets knotted together had been left there, so he must have thought he would need them to get back into the room. And then? Who did he meet? Whoever it was, Ernst Äbi must have gone with him, so it must have been a man who had power over him. Very great power for, if you continued the train of thought and assumed the student had been taken to the glasshouse and pushed into the section filled with poisonous gas, he could easily have broken the glass in the top half of the door with his fist. One sharp blow would have saved him. Why had he stayed in the place with the lethal gas? Why had he allowed himself to be locked in?

Just a minute. He had no proof whatsoever that Ernst Äbi had been locked in. No proof? Some suspicious circumstances, though. Firstly: someone had exchanged the rusty key for a new one? Why? Secondly: Arnold Äbi, the dead man's father, possessed a vice that was attached to the kitchen table and was covered in iron filings. And there was something else, a third suspicious circumstance. Studer thought and thought, his brow furrowed in concentration. Then the furrows cleared. "Aah!" was all the sergeant said. He remembered that Frau Äbi had complained about some tablets that were missing. Tablets that were clearly narcotic.

Studer gave Arnold Äbi a hard look, but when he saw the expression on the man's face, he realized he would get nowhere at the moment. There would be no point in searching his pockets, presumably by now the key had long been concealed somewhere. There were enough places here where it could be hidden: large flowerpots, a pile of sand in one corner, peat in another; the table running down the middle of the glasshouse was in two parts and one part was enclosed with six-inch planks and piled up with soil; there were plants growing that Studer didn't even know the name of; and sawdust everywhere. Impossible to tell if the sawdust had recently been used to conceal something. Studer was sure he wouldn't find anything in the drunkard's room either ('drunkard" was what Studer called Äbi in his own mind). The "narcotic" had probably been dumped with the rubbish by now – and the three locales had no lack of that.

Despite the expression that covered the old man's face like a mask – his lips and eyes were full of scorn – the sergeant decided it was worth one attempt. He said out loud, "I would very much like to search Ernst Äbi's desk."

"What? Tonight?" the principal asked, and Paul Wottli protested as well. Indeed, he protested so strongly it aroused Studer's suspicion, for he had clearly seen the somewhat questioning looks both of them had given Äbi as they spoke. Arnold Äbi's expression changed almost immediately. The scorn

110

vanished; his eyelids were lowered. Then he shook his head, his cheeks had turned pale. Was the man afraid?

"I insist on it," Studer said. "And I have one further question, Herr Wottli. How many copies of the glass-house key are there?"

"Which key do you mean? The one to the main door? There's only one of that, this one here." Wottli took his key ring out of his pocket and held up a middle-sized key.

Studer shook his head. "I mean the key to *this* door," he said, pointing at the door to the section that had been fumigated.

"Two," said Wottli quietly. Why did he keep looking at Äbi out of the corner of his eye? "The principal has one, and I have the other."

"Where is your key, Herr Direktor?"

"In my office. In one of the desk drawers."

"And to whom does this one belong?"

They both spoke at the same time, pushing forward – and Arnold Äbi hid behind them. What was the old drunkard doing there? Why was he hiding? Studer just had time to see that the man was wearing gloves.

"It could be mine." – "That's the principal's."

A duet is only pleasant to hear when it's a song that's being sung; words spoken by two voices, on the other hand, make your ears ache.

"Just a moment." Studer raised his hands. "One at a time, please. You are sure the key is yours, are you, Principal? Quite sure? When was the last time you used it?"

"That I couldn't say. A few days ago – perhaps a week . . . Oh, now I remember. I gave it to Ernst Äbi exactly a week ago, last Thursday. He didn't give it back to me until Sunday, claiming he had simply forgotten."

"And yours, Herr Wottli?"

"It's been in my pocket all the time."

"Why not on your key ring?"

"Because I have to give it to a student now and then. No one needs the one to the outside door, that's always open, except during the holidays."

"Ludwig," Studer called. The young man was hiding in a dark corner. Now he came over. "Can you remember what the key you saw in the lock inside was like?"

Silence. Ludwig's eyes went from one to the other. Arnold Äbi's head appeared over the principal's shoulder, his eyelids wide apart. How he was staring at the lad!

"I . . . I don't know . . . It . . . it looked old and rusty."

"Older than this one?"

"But that one's new."

"Silence." – "Shut up." – "Liar." – "Just what you'd expect from someone who's been in the reformatory."

"Quiet!" Studer roared. Then he said, with a malicious smile, "Strange how people can get worked up over a simple key." While they were shouting at Ludwig, Arnold Äbi's face had gone bright red; at Studer's words it went pale. The sergeant just managed to register that before his head disappeared behind Sack-Amherd's back once more. The two others also seemed to realize they had made a mistake. Fear crept into their minds and changed their expressions.

"This is more than a body can bear, Sergeant, you're making us quite nervous. Do you think we are enjoying this? First of all you suspect one of our students, search his locker and find bloodstained clothing so that it looks as if the lad must at least have been party to a murder, even if he didn't commit it himself. You make Ernst Äbi so worried that he commits suicide that very same evening. And what are you trying to make it into now? Even the first case here you made into – er . . .

112

made out to be a murder, despite the contrary opinion of the local doctor. And now you're saying Ernst Äbi was murdered? By whom? I saw myself that the key was in the lock on the inside. It's impossible for someone to have locked the door from outside when the key is on the inside – I repeat: on the inside. Is that not so?"

"Then why are the small pliers missing?" Studer asked, so quietly that the principal leaned forward and put his right hand behind his ear. The sergeant repeated his question a little louder.

"Small pliers? But we haven't got that kind of pliers. Moreover, Sergeant, you cannot prove that some other key was used. Or are you maintaining that the key that was found on the floor had been exchanged by someone? If that is what you think, then I must beg to differ. In my opinion, the matter is clear: Ernst Äbi returned the key to me and saw where I put it away. What is more likely than that the student took it from my desk this evening – in order to commit suicide?"

The Principal had hardly finished than the sergeant saw the drunkard reappear. He stood directly underneath the light, crossed his arms and stared at Studer with wide-open eyes.

Studer began to have doubts. Strange: Arnold Äbi was respectably dressed, you could tell that his wife kept everything neat and tidy. His suit was old, but the collar of his jacket wasn't greasy, it had been well brushed, and his light blue shirt was clean. And yet . . . and yet . . . There was an expression on the man's face . . . It was no longer scornful, yet there was something of the poorhouse about it.

But – you can dislike the way a man looks, that doesn't prove he murdered his son. To prove that you would have to assume the key had been exchanged. Who by? It didn't have to be Arnold Äbi. It could just as well have been Sack-Amherd, Wottli or even Ludwig. The three of them had been there all the time, and two had protested strongly against the suggestion of an exchange.

He needed to find a motive strong enough to make one of them commit murder. Was there such a motive?

God forbid! It wouldn't be the first time Studer heard of a father killing his son. The reason? Ernst Äbi would surely have been named in the Chinaman's will. If he were eliminated, the other heirs would profit by it. The others? It was not only the drunkard who had an interest, through his wife; there was also Hungerlott, the warden, through his dead wife. Ludwig would have to be included too. And then Ernst's teacher, Wottli.

The sergeant was tired. He saw that it was already a quarter past eleven. Most of all he would have liked to arrest all those standing around in the glasshouse, without a by-your-leave – or to tell them to go to the devil. But that was out of the question, so he asked Sack-Amherd to take him back to the college building for a moment. There were two things he wanted to see, he explained: the drawer where the other key had been kept and the dead man's desk. Paul Wottli was asked to accompany Ernst's father back to the poorhouse and then to go home.

"Ludwig," he said, finally turning to Ernst's stepbrother, "you're to stay here. You're to guard the glasshouse until I come back to fetch you. Understood? And you, Herr Wottli, will give me the key to the outside door? Take it off your key ring. *Meerci.* And now let's go, Herr Sack-Amherd . . ."

Students at night

The ground floor of the school was brightly lit, and there were still some lights on up on the second floor. As Studer entered the vestibule with the principal, it made him think of an enormous beehive. The whole building was filled with a loud buzzing that was muted, but not completely silenced, by the closed doors of the classrooms.

Sack-Amherd went into his office and switched on the light. A huge desk by the window, an iron safe by the door and shelves on the walls filled with box files . . . Sack-Amherd, disgruntled, sat down in the chair at his desk, pulled out an unlocked drawer and started to rummage round in it. Papers fluttered to the floor. Then he opened a second drawer, searched through it, and a third . . .

"The key's gone," he sighed.

Studer nodded silently.

"But that's clear proof," the principal went on, "that the dead man came into my office and stole the key because he intended to commit suicide. Isn't it?"

Studer shrugged his shoulders and plunged his hands deeper into his trouser pockets.

"Proof?" he murmured. "I see no proof. First of all we have to establish when Äbi took the key. This evening? Or earlier on? During the day? And are you quite sure your key was new, Herr Direktor? Was it really this key?" He took the shiny object out of his pocket and held it under Sack-Amherd's nose. The principal yawned.

"How should I know? I haven't seen the key for ages. – Ah, now I remember. When Äbi asked for it last week, I simply told him to go and fetch it and explained which drawer it was in. He brought it back and put it away himself and only told me he'd done so afterwards. I can't waste my time on minor matters like that. Do you still want to go and see his desk?"

They went out into the corridor and headed for a door diagonally opposite the principal's office.

"Just wait a moment," he said quietly, putting his hand on the principal's arm to stop him.

In the classroom a voice was saying, "Do you really think that sergeant, that copper, is going to find anything, Baumann? Instead of asking us, he tacks on to the old man and Wottli. As if either of them had any idea about Äbi. I know more about Äbi than the rest of the college put together, believe you me."

"Shh! Shhh!" the others chorused. "Not so loud." – "If someone should be listening!" – "I'll just open the door and have a look . . ."

Studer didn't wait but turned the handle.

It was bright as day in the classroom, the four lamps in the ceiling must have had very strong bulbs. Three rows of desks with seats attached; immediately opposite the door a long, wide table for the teacher; the blackboard on the wall with something sketched in chalk on it, the plan of a building – good God, it was the glasshouse. Beside it was a smaller sketch that excited Studer's curiosity.

"What's this you've drawn here?" he asked drumming his fingers on the blackboard. The reply came from a chorus of at least twenty voices: "the heating system."

"Which heating system?"

"The glasshouse's."

116

Of course! The lads weren't stupid. They'd thought of the heating system – and a trained detective felt ashamed of himself because he'd forgotten such an important factor. Studer did not hesitate.

"I don't need you any more, Herr Direktor. I can see you're very tired, off you go to your bed. I can handle these students, don't you worry." – Studer spoke very softly, close to Sack-Amherd's ear and holding his hand by his mouth. – "And I'll make sure they go up to the dormitories afterwards."

"Fine. If you say so." The principal gave another wide yawn. It was so quiet in the room a knocking could be heard that came from the ceiling. "Yes, that's my wife calling me. I'm sure she's worried. So . . . I wish you all good night. And – don't make too much noise."

Herr Sack-Amherd closed the door quietly behind him, the sound of his steps faded. There was silence in the classroom.

"Right," said Studer, taking off his coat, "let's do this investigation together. Who was it talking to Baumann before I came in?"

"Me." A tall fellow stood up in the back row, right at the top. His hair gleamed red, and his face was covered in freckles.

"What's your name?"

"Amstein. Walter Amstein."

"Right then, Wälti – I presume that's not what your teachers call you, but that's the way I do things. I presume you don't mind?"

"No, not at all. In fact, I prefer it." And the redhead laughed, showing a row of fine teeth.

"What did you mean, Wälti, by saying you knew more about Äbi than the rest of the college put together? I heard that out in the corridor."

"You see, I was right," a small, brown-haired lad

shouted to Amstein. He'd taken off his jacket and rolled up his sleeves.

"Are you Baumann?" Studer asked.

"Mmm." The lad nodded. The muscles at his elbows were tensed; he had his hands clasped round his chin. "I know you, Sergeant. I was in The Sun on the eighteenth, and I saw the poorhouse lot try to beat you up."

Studer took that up and questioned Baumann. "What was the reason? I never really got to the bottom of it. After all, it was pure chance that I'd forgotten to fill up and –"

He was interrupted by three students at once: by Baumann, Amstein and a third, whose hair was almost white like an albino's. He had horn-rimmed glasses, and the lenses were so strong, the eyes behind them were completely distorted. His name was Popingha, and he spoke German with a strong Dutch accent. He ordered the others to shut up and told the following story:

On that evening Ernst Äbi had suddenly come into the classroom and said he needed four men. He (Popingha) and Amstein and Heinis and Vonzugarten had gone with him. On the way Ernst had told them that his brother – his stepbrother – had arrived that morning. Some time before, the Poor Board had sent him to the poorhouse, but he had run off with a girl. The stranger, Farny, had taken him under his wing, but with Hungerlott you never knew what the man had up his sleeve. That morning he'd agreed not to do anything about his brother, Ernst had said, and he'd promised Farny that too. But in the evening a policeman had suddenly turned up, perhaps he was going to arrest his brother. He'd managed to get some of the poorhouse inmates together, but he needed a few more he could rely on, which was why he'd come to us.

We were to frighten the cop, he said, so he'd go and leave Ludwig in peace.

"That's the way it was, Sergeant, that's why we behaved as if we were going to attack you."

How simple it was when you knew the story! And how brave the lad had been, the lad who was now lying dead in the glasshouse, guarded by his stepbrother.

The glasshouse . . . what was the point of the plan of the heating system?

This time it was Amstein who answered. His bed, he explained, was next to Äbi's in the dormitory. He had noticed that recently Äbi had been sleeping badly. Often he had lain awake almost the whole night and when he finally dropped off towards morning, he had talked in his sleep. He kept going on about the boiler room. The boiler room and the glasshouse. A few times Ernst, Baumann's best friend – "that's right isn't it, Buuma?" – "Sure!" – a few times Ernst had skipped evening study. They had study in the college in the morning from half past six until breakfast at half past seven – earlier in the summer – and in the evening from five until half past six and from half past seven until ten. He just mentioned that to put the sergeant in the picture . . . So Baumann had told him that Äbi was sometimes missing, and since Baumann was shy he, Amstein, had followed Äbi. And what had he discovered? Ernst had met his father out in the graveyard.

"The two of them were standing by the grave of Frau Hungerlott, who had died a fortnight previously. I knew that she was Ernst's sister, what I couldn't understand was why he should be meeting his father there. Afterwards the two of them went to the glasshouse. At first I stayed outside, then I went in. There was no one there, but I could hear them whispering, down in the boiler room. I couldn't hear what they were saying, though. Then I slipped away. There was just one strange thing: the bulb down in the boiler room was off all that night, but last Monday I saw a light down there. It was around nine, and Äbi was on duty that week; in the morning he had to clear out the grid and in the evening build up the fire for the night ... I thought Äbi must have a spare bulb, which he took out when he left the boiler room and replaced with another, an old one that didn't work. Why he should do that I've no idea."

A second discovery. Studer deliberately did not make notes. There is nothing more off-putting than pedantic note-taking – and while you're doing that, you can't look up and you lose completely the rapport with the person you're listening to. For a while there was silence. All the students were flushed, their eyes sparkling.

"Anything else?"

Popingha, the Dutchman with the thick glasses, gave a short laugh and nodded. He knew something else, he said, but he didn't think it was important.

"Come on then, tell me." Actually Studer was surprised how well he was getting on with these students who were strangers to him. They should have hated him because that morning he had searched Äbi's locker and found a piece of incriminating evidence. They all seemed so devastated by the death of their fellow student that they had overcome their natural reserve and wanted to help.

Popingha came out with his revelation: he regularly used to see Frau Anna Hungerlott out walking with their teacher, Herr Wottli, and he was willing to bet they'd been in love with each other.

Studer was about to smile, he could feel the corners of his mouth twitch, but suddenly he felt a shiver, even though it was stiflingly hot in the classroom. He felt he'd caught hold of the end of the thread and now he could unravel the tangled, knotted skein.

"Off you go to bed now," he commanded. "And go up the stairs quietly."

The students followed him. He put out the lights, waited on the second floor until they were all in bed, then put out the lights in the dormitories as well.

"Goodnight, sleep tight."

When he left the building it was a quarter to one. The glasshouse was still brightly lit.

Finds in the boiler room

As Studer entered the corridor to the two greenhouses he saw Ludwig Farny standing by the cement table. He was picking up sand in his right hand and letting it trickle into his left hand; tears were running down his cheeks. The sergeant went up to him, patted him on the shoulder and asked, "What's the matter?"

Haltingly Ludwig told him that Ernst had always stood by him. As he spoke, he pointed to the dead body lying in the darkness. Once, he said, when he was having a difficult time and Barbara was ill, he'd written to Ernst for money. Fifty francs he'd asked for, and Ernst had sent him the money without further ado, even though he wasn't well off himself. And then Ernst always protected their mother and when he was at home his father – his stepfather – had never dared lay a hand on her. There had even been a fight once, he went on, because old Äbi had been drunk and had started to go on at their mother. At the time Ernst had only been sixteen, but he was strong as an ox and the next morning his father had had a black eye.

"That'll do for the moment," said Studer. Could one imagine a better motive? The old man must have hated his son. Studer knew that type, men who, when they were drunk, liked to torment their wives. There must be some need for power behind it, since the tormentors were usually poor wretches. They were downtrodden, no wonder they bullied their wives to show them how strong they were.

"Do you know where the boiler room is, Ludwig?"
The lad nodded and led the way. In one corner some
steps led down into the basement. Ludwig turned on a
switch – a light went on down below. Ernst must have
changed the bulb before he died . . .

The boiler was dusty; to the right of it was a heap of
ashes mixed with cinders. In the adjoining room on
the left was a pile of coke. Studer took off his coat and
hung it on a nail. Among several pairs of overalls he
found one that fitted and put it on. There was a riddle
leaning against the wall. "We're going to have to sieve
the ashes, Ludwig," the sergeant said. "Put one of
those on over your clothes." He was assuming Ludwig
was wearing his one and only Sunday suit.

It was an unpleasant task they had undertaken. The
air in the small room was soon thick with dust, breath-
ing was difficult, and it made Studer cough. But the
heap was getting smaller – although the sergeant did
not really know what he hoped to find in it. Ludwig
swept up the last of the ashes, the two men shook the
riddle and finally, among the cinders, the sergeant
found three objects: a half-burnt button, a whole button and a burnt-out cartridge case. Studer put the
three objects in the palm of his hand and looked
at them.

"You see that button, Ludwig?" he said. "That's from
a department store. While this one," – he pointed at
the undamaged button – "is good quality, a coat button, perhaps even from an English tailor. And do you
recognize that?"

Ludwig nodded. When he was a boy he'd picked up
cartridge cases like that at the firing range, he said.
Only those'd been bigger. If he might venture an opinion, he'd say it was a cartridge case from a handgun, a
large-calibre gun.

123

"Quite right, Ludwig, quite right. The cartridge probably came from the American revolver we found by your uncle's hand in the graveyard."

Ludwig nodded sagely. A smile appeared on his gaunt face, and his blue eyes shone.

Studer had switched on his torch and was sweeping the beam round the walls. He stopped beside the entrance to the coal cellar, went up until his eyes were close to the wall.

"Come and have a look," he cried. Ludwig came over, and the sergeant pointed to some splashes that were clearly visible against the dark wall.

"Have you got an old knife?" he asked his assistant. Ludwig nodded, although it took him some time before he could extract a knife with a notched blade from his trouser pocket.

Studer took out an old envelope and scratched off the wall covering with the suspicious splashes. Then he sealed the envelope and treated his assistant to a lecture:

The way he imagined it was as follows, he said. Ludwig's uncle had been lured to the boiler room. And he'd been got out of bed. Proof? The button from a good tailor. His uncle had probably thrown a coat over his pyjamas and followed the man who had called him. That man knew that your uncle always carried a gun. How the murderer had managed to get the gun off him was a mystery that would presumably not be solved until the murderer made his confession. To cut a long story short, James Farny had been shot, there in that boiler room, with a small-bore gun, but the big revolver had also been fired. And they had to assume that there had not been just the one murderer – at least one accomplice must have been present. The accomplice had gone to Farny's room and brought a shirt, a suit and a collar. They dressed the dead body in the boiler room, carried it to the graveyard and placed it on Anna Hungerlott's grave. Ludwig should bear in mind that their intention was to get the authorities to think it was suicide caused by a lover's sorrow. But they had made a mistake. They had forgotten that the coat, waistcoat and shirt were undamaged. The deputy governor had immediately pointed out that it was impossible for a man with a bullet through his heart to button up his clothes.

"Their first mistake, Ludwig. If they'd thought a little, they could have avoided it. We won't talk about their second mistake – the key – just now. You're tired, and Sergeant Studer's an old gasbag. Let's get some sleep. Come on . . ." They went up the steps, Ludwig turned off the light. The corridor was empty. The runes Studer had traced hours ago in the peat piled up on the cement table were still there. He rubbed them out and the coolness felt good on his hot hand. By the outside door Ludwig turned off the last switch. Now the glasshouse was dark; inside Ernst lay undisturbed, sleeping the lonely sleep of the dead, while the two living men set off for their beds, after Studer had locked the outside door. The moon had already set and the sky shimmered with a faint, silvery glow. When Studer took out his pocket watch, he saw that it was two hours after midnight.

A nocturnal visit from the lawyer

Kindness can have its inconveniences. When Studer invited Ludwig Farny to sleep in the same room, he did not know that the lad snored. He had only realized that during the previous night. Now it started up again. Scarcely had the sergeant put out the light than a groaning, sawing, rasping, snorting started up in the bed on the other side of the room. Studer threw his slipper across. For a minute there was silence, then the noise began again. The other slipper flew across the room, then the right shoe, the left shoe, one leather gaiter, the other leather gaiter. The silence on the other side of the room never lasted more than a minute. With a sigh Studer rolled over onto his other side, gritted his teeth, began to count, said his multiplication tables out loud ... Ludwig continued to snore. The clock in the tower of the horticultural college struck half past two, the tinny bell of the poorhouse replied, they struck a quarter to, they struck three o'clock. Groaning, the sergeant switched the light back on and started to read the bits of the newspaper he'd missed.

The shutters were closed; their green wood shimmered through the windowpanes. The light in the room did not bother the young man. Suddenly Studer sat up with a start. He had the feeling someone had knocked at the door. He waited. Then he saw the handle pushed down from outside. Someone was trying to open the door – thank God it was locked.

Studer got out of bed and crept to the door. He pressed his ear against the wood, but he could hear nothing. Any noise was drowned out by Ludwig's snores. Finally a soft voice outside enquired, "Studer, are you still awake?" It was the voice of Münch, the lawyer! The sergeant pushed back the bolt, unlocked the door and let his friend in.

"Don't make too much noise," he told the lawyer, "there's someone sleeping in the other bed. He's a good lad, he's done his bit today and earned his sleep ... He does rather snore, but then no one's perfect."

While he was speaking, Studer slipped back into bed and invited the lawyer to sit on it. Münch accepted his invitation, demanded a pillow, claiming the wall was hard, stuffed it behind his back and said, "Getting out of the poorhouse wasn't easy."

Studer showed no sympathy. He laughed and said it was healthy for lawyers to get a bit of exercise now and then. As it was, they spent all their time sitting at their desks cheating their clients.

Münch responded by pinching Studer's calf, but his riposte got him nowhere because Studer suddenly stretched out his long legs and squashed his friend mercilessly against the foot of the bed until Münch begged for mercy.

What was he doing here so late? Studer asked in a whisper – although the whispering was unnecessary, Ludwig continued to snore undisturbed. Had something happened, over there in the poorhouse? And, anyway, what was a lawyer doing visiting Hungerlott? As far as he – Studer – was aware, the warden wasn't exactly pure as the driven snow.

"Wouldn't you like to know that, eh?" said Münch, twisting and craning his neck in his high collar.

"Know! Trying to play the private investigator, are we?

There's no complaint been made against Hungerlott so far, but as I understand it, you think the warden poisoned his wife with arsenic. Now if I should tell you we found one of the students at the college possessed the poison, what would you say then? And if I also tell you that yesterday that same student sent a warning: 'Keep your fingers off our *rösti*' smashing through my window, what would you say to that?"

"That you're a mooncalf," the lawyer said dryly.

"An old joke," said Studer grumpily. " 'Mooncalf' is what deputy governors and doctors call each other in Pfründisberg. Are you going to follow their example?"

You could tell, said the lawyer, that it was a long time since the sergeant had won at billiards; losing always had a deleterious effect on his mental faculties. Studer muttered an insult, then asked to what he owed the honour of such a late visit?

"Today," said Münch, "you were in the Institute for Forensic Medicine. What did the tests on the hand-kerchiefs show?"

"For a lawyer you're not as stupid as you look," said Studer dryly. "Come on, out with it."

Münch undid his coat, took a letter out of his wallet. "There, read that," he said.

Studer read it:

Pfründisberg
17 November 19—

Dear Herr Münch,

Shortly after the death of my niece, Anna Hungerlott-Äbi, I made the following change to my will: the quarter of my estate that was to go to my niece was to be divided into two parts, one to go to Anna's husband, Hungerlott, the warden of the poorhouse, and the other to Paul Wottli, a teacher at Pfründisberg Horticultural College. I find myself compelled to change this new clause, and I would ask you to come and see me tomorrow, 18 November, at 10 am. I would also ask you to bring my will, since I intend to replace it with a new one. I have already written a draft so that it will not take long. I beg you not to be late. A few days ago I told one of my acquaintances of this intended change and I am afraid he immediately spread the news around. The fact that other people know of my intention means my life is doubly endangered. A few months ago I chanced to make the acquaintance of one of your friends and told him then that my life was in danger. This friend of yours, Sergeant Jakob Studer, was somewhat sceptical about my claim. It therefore seemed advisable to turn to you, since you are a friend of the policeman. I would be very grateful if you would bring in Sergeant Studer, should anything happen to me. I am telling you this because it seemed necessary to explain briefly why I have turned to you in order to make my will.

Until tomorrow.

Yours faithfully

James Farny.

Studer examined the letter from all sides; it was typewritten.

"I'm sure he'll have kept a copy."

"So am I," the lawyer agreed.

"But I didn't find the copy among his things."

"Nor did I," said the lawyer innocently.

129

"Oh, so you searched the room, did you?"

Münch shrugged his shoulders. "I just happened to get there before the police. It does sometimes happen that lawyers get up before detectives . . ."

Studer scratched his neck, at a loss. His nightshirt – the collar was embroidered with little red flowers – was open, revealing his powerful chest.

"Was the body already on the grave when you arrived?" he asked.

Again the lawyer shrugged his shoulders. "Unfortunately, I can't help you there. I went straight to the inn and asked for Farny's room. The waitress showed me there, and then I just waited – until twelve o'clock. Eventually I got fed up with waiting, and the police were making a racket in the inn, so I went over to the poorhouse. You should have seen the welcome I got! The warden asked me to stay, put a room at my disposal, invited me to lunch. I'd never have thought you could have such a good lunch in the poorhouse. He was very friendly, was Hungerlott, and lamented bitterly the loss of his wife. And I have to say losing your wife is very hard indeed . . ."

Studer looked at his friend. The lawyer was smiling, and it would have been a definite exaggeration to call it a sympathetic smile.

"Gastric influenza!" Münch said. "Gastric influenza . . . that name can hide a multitude of sins, don't you think, Studer?"

"Hmm," Studer muttered. "The Marsh test was pretty clear . . . and Dr Malapelle in Forensic was sure."

"Arsenic?" Münch asked. "Hmm, hmm."

It would have been very quiet in the room, had it not been for Ludwig Farny's resounding snores.

"You've got a good alarm clock there," said Münch, pointing with his thumb at the other bed.

130

Studer sighed. "He's not had a great life, you know. He was put into service with a farmer as a boy, then he came into Hungerlott's tender care, ran off and lived in the woods with a girl. Perhaps he'll come into some money now . . . I wouldn't begrudge it him."

"Me neither," said Münch. Then he picked up his wallet again, took out a handwritten document and handed it to Studer. In brief, it said that James Farny, born on such and such a date, place of origin Gampligen, bequeathed his estate, consisting of English and American currency as well as precious stones kept in a safe-deposit box at the Crédit Lyonnais, in equal parts to his sister, Elisa, the wife of Arnold Äbi, to her illegitimate son, Ludwig Farny, and to her legitimate children, Ernst and Anna. Should one of the four die before the death of the testator, the estate was to be divided up among the remaining heirs. Arnold Äbi, the husband of Elisa, née Farny, had no claim on the inheritance. A codicil dated 10 November contained the following clause: the husband of his niece, Anna, would inherit his wife's portion, if she should die; half of it, however, was to be handed on to Paul Wottli, a teacher at Pfründisberg Horticultural College. The executor was Münch.

"The will is dated 25 July," said Studer. "Were you there when it was drawn up?"

Münch nodded. He had his hands clasped round his shins, and his chin was rubbing against his drawn-up knees.

"On 25 July," he said reflectively. "I never really managed to explain it. Why, for example, had James Farny come to me? Why did he mention you? Who had told him we were friends? Do you remember we played billiards together, Jakob, on the 20th and the 21st, in our usual café? Did anything strike you on either evening?"

131

Studer suppressed a yawn. Then he shook his head. "When I'm playing billiards," he said in bored tones, "I forget my profession. I'm not going to check who's watching when I'm making a ten-point break, am I?"

"I realize that," said Münch. "that's why I didn't tell you that Farny came to see me on the 25th, at eleven in the morning, and questioned me about you first. He wanted to know all kinds of things. Whether you'd been successful in your career, why you'd only made it to sergeant and more along the same lines. So I sang your praises and said that the only people who got on in this country were people who belonged to some political party. Studer had never belonged to any party, on the contrary! Once he'd ended up with egg all over his face because of some business with a bank that was meant to be hushed up because a few well-known people had been compromised in it. 'Aha!' Farny had said to that, 'that's interesting.' – 'Not for Studer,' I said, 'because he lost his job and had to start from scratch again.' Studer, I told him, would probably never get beyond sergeant. In the first place he hadn't got any relatives (in Switzerland we call nepotism 'nephewism') and in the second place we like to keep competent people in subordinate positions and only use them when it's absolutely necessary. Then we can order them around, so everything's OK. 'So if it's a complicated case, Studer will be put in charge of the investigation?' Farny asked. – 'Yes,' I said, 'I can guarantee that. They assign him to such cases on his own until they're solved, and the superintendent at CID as well as the Chief of Police support him and let him do as he likes. Then he's shunted off into the sidings again for a rest . . .' – 'Oh,' Farny said, 'that's interesting. I think that's the way things are all over the world. Good, let's draw up that will.'

"He told me what he wanted, I dictated it to him and he wrote it down. Then he left the will with me. Before he went, as he had his hand on the doorknob, he said he would probably be murdered. By one of his relatives, by one of his acquaintances, it was all uncertain. But he could have been killed twice already, if he hadn't been used to keeping his eye open. Yes . . . That's what I wanted to tell you."

"*Meerci*, Hans." It was only rarely that the sergeant called his friend by his first name, and today he found it particularly difficult because he remembered that the cock that had been dissected had been called Hans too. And he felt something like fear welling up inside him. Hadn't one man already died because he knew too much? Äbi, the student at the horticultural college? Was the lawyer in danger?

"Listen, Hans," he said, "you just watch out nothing happens to you. D'you understand?"

"Yes, yes. Don't you worry."

"So the will says that Farny's estate is to be divided up into four parts. That's right, isn't it? Two of the heirs have died, which means that Ludwig, who's had such a bad time of it, will inherit one half and his mother the other."

"Wrong! You're tired, Jakob. You can't count. It's to be divided up into three: Ludwig Farny, Elisa Äbi and Vinzenz Hungerlott. And the warden's share is to be divided up, Wottli's to get half of that."

"Does Wottli know that?"

"From Farny's letter it sounds likely. But it may be that only Hungerlott knows and Wottli doesn't. So, now I'm off. Have a good sleep."

Could he keep the letter and the will? Studer asked. Münch nodded. Then, as a kind of finale to his nocturnal visit, he added, "You know, Jakob, as things stood, I wouldn't have been able to come to see you before this evening. The Warden hasn't let me out of his sight ever since I arrived yesterday. I was given a room that was next to his bedroom and only had one door. If I wanted to go out I had to go past Hungerlott's bed. But I was moved this evening because a new guest arrived, and he must be very important, because I've been forgotten. That's how I managed to slip out."

Again Studer was overcome with the inexplicable feeling of fear. "Take care, Hans," he said, and the lawyer gave him an astonished look.

"What could happen to me?" he asked.

Studer shrugged his shoulders. Then he got up and accompanied his friend to the door.

"Just don't fall down the stairs, right?" Münch just laughed.

Studer lay in his bed (it was nice to be able to stretch out at last), stared at the light and thought . . . He must be careful not to jump to conclusions. After all, even though Hungerlott's wife had died, it did not make him any better off. It was a complicated business. He'd played cards with Hungerlott that evening and established that the man played well. He needed a trump up his sleeve, for it had been easy to see that the warden played well, he played his cards according to plan, not at random. If he knew what was in the will, then surely he would have some countermove ready to put Wottli out of the reckoning. After all, a man does not risk twenty years in jail for poison merely to get his hands on a fortune he knows he's going to have to share. Studer's mind was quite clear, and the snoring of his roommate did not disturb him in the least; it was more like a pleasant musical accompaniment to his thinking.

And there was one more thing he had to remember:

members of parliament and doctors were coming to visit the poorhouse in the morning. Was that his trump?

Just a minute! He must be careful not to make the mistake of concentrating on the one suspect. Wottli also had an interest in the inheritance. He might be a pleasant enough fellow who had worked his way up and looked after his old mother, but that didn't mean he was innocent. Some things pointed to him. The inheritance from the man by Lake Thun, for example. The bloodstained pyjamas that had been wrapped up in paper with *his* address on it – and the address had been scored out. And who knew that the glasshouse was being fumigated with hydrogen cyanide gas? The teacher, Herr Wottli. Who always had the key to the glasshouse on him? Wottli. The only thing in his favour was the fact that his motive was not clear. What could have driven the teacher to commit two murders? But, after all, *he* was the one who had the new preparation for a plant disinfectant in his possession, *he* was testing it out . . . Could one not imagine that he had fallen in love with Frau Hungerlott, been rejected and poisoned her out of revenge? And if some of the students knew, then Ernst Äbi would know more than most. Had he known what was going on? Perhaps Ludwig knew something?

"Ludwig!" The snoring grew quieter. "Ludwig!"

He sat up in bed. "Eh? Has something happened?"

"Listen, lad. Did you notice anything suggesting Wottli was in love with Frau Hungerlott?"

Ludwig rubbed his eyes. At first he couldn't understand what Studer was going on about, and the sergeant had to repeat his question three times. Finally he cottoned on. Yes, on that 18 July he'd seen the two of them; they'd been out for a walk together.

What kind of woman had Frau Hungerlott been? the sergeant wanted to know.

"Beautiful!" The lad's eyes shone. A fine figure, he said. She'd also been strict, but she'd always worn fine clothes, and she often used to go to the hairdresser's in Bern to get her hair done, and she used to paint her fingernails . . .

"Oh, and one other thing. She did the bookkeeping."

"Aha . . . Did she now? The bookkeeping," said Studer. This time his yawn was loud and long, a yawn without any ulterior motive. He felt his eyelids grow heavy.

"Don't snore too much, Ludwig."

"No, Sergeant."

"And put the light out." Five minutes later both were asleep, and neither disturbed the other. In fact, it would have been difficult to say whose snoring was the louder, the sergeant's or Ludwig Farny's.

Wottli decides to leave

Studer's last thoughts before he fell asleep were: "The case is so far advanced that to hurry would only harm things." So he decided to have a long sleep. He and his assistant did not appear downstairs until nine o'clock. The old innkeeper was sitting at a table, studying the newspaper through a pair of bent steel-rimmed glasses. When the sergeant appeared in the doorway, Brönnimann greeted him with a friendly grin.

"Pfründisberg's gettin' famous," he squawked. "Two murders, Sergeant, two murders! Yes, Pfründisberg's gettin' famous, just like it used to be, in my grand-father's day. Then it was called 'Bad Pfründisberg', and the gentlemen from the city came to take the waters. But then, of course, the government bought up the monastery and turned it into a poorhouse – and the fine ladies and gentlemen stopped coming. Rich people don't like to see scroungers around, you know, Sergeant. And since then The Sun's turned into a boozer where the poorhouse men come for their cheap schnapps. Now and then there's a funeral meal here, when someone from Gampligen dies and gets buried in the graveyard over there. Otherwise there's just the students come for a glass of beer. Sack-Amherd don't like it, he'd rather come by 'imself and play *Jass* with the warden, Schranz and Gerber. I join in myself, now and then, if they need me, but I'm gettin' on, you know, I can't see the cards that well and, anyway, in my day we used to play the kind where clubs is always trumps, not this silly variant where you have to choose. The best is when Hungerlott, Sack-Amherd and Schranz play *Zuger Jass* for five rappen a point. That's when you see how these fine gentlemen can swear ... Do you know some people are coming to inspect the poorhouse tomorrow?"

"Yes, I did hear," Studer growled, "but now I want some strong coffee, none of your chicory stuff, and butter and cheese. Where's Huldi?"

The innkeeper called the waitress himself, and in five minutes the girl with the pale complexion had brought his order. You could see how proud Ludwig was to be sitting at the same table as the sergeant. The lad was on his best behaviour, he didn't drop his food, didn't put too-large chunks in his mouth and didn't eat off his knife very often. He didn't slurp his coffee either.

At half past nine they were finished and left, saying goodbye to the innkeeper. On the way to the college the sergeant made a speech to his protégé:

He could see how things were always changing in the world. That tavern, for example, once it had been a smart hostelry. Ludwig should just imagine it: the chaises, the brakes that used to stop here, men and women in fine clothes had gone in, stayed in the rooms that were empty now, a playground for rats and mice ... In its place the state had opened two institutions. One was a new building; the other had stayed the same as when the monks had built it five, who knows, perhaps six hundred years ago. In the college gardeners were being trained – the future unemployed; in the other the poor, who were of no use any more, were fed with a bit of soup and coffee so that at least they didn't die of starvation in the streets ... He was having a very philosophical morning, was Sergeant

Studer of the Cantonal Criminal Investigation Department . . . He always felt, he went on, that there was
something sad about these poorhouses. He remembered in France, in Paris especially, there were poor
people there too, but at least they kept a person's most
priceless possession: their freedom. The police turned
a blind eye when they saw one of them begging. In the
winter, when it was cold, the poor sat on the steps of
the underground stations at night to get at least some
warmth and wait for the day. The nights were short in
the big city, he said, at four in the morning already you
could see the poor at the markets, helping the market
gardeners, who came with early vegetables, to unload
their carts, there was a little money in it for them – and
something to eat. During the day they went round
the streets and people weren't really mean, especially
the workers, here a franc, there a few sous. Here
in Switzerland, on the other hand . . . The sergeant
didn't want to say anything against his own country,
but this round-the-clock charity had always got on his
nerves.

Tiny white clouds were creeping across a deep blue
sky; a gentle breeze was playing with the dry grass by
the edge of the path. The sergeant was in a good
mood, and Ludwig's eyes, those eyes of a remarkable,
shining blue, were fixed on him. The young man
seemed to be drinking in his words: no one had ever
spoken to him like this before, confirming ideas that
sometimes came to him. And now a middle-aged man,
whose thin face did not really go with his massive phys-
ique, was walking beside him, putting these thoughts
into words, thoughts which until now had just crept
round inside his head like larvae, giving shape to them
and sending them fluttering off through the air like
colourful butterflies . . .

"*Meerci*," said Ludwig. Studer turned to look at him, saw the pleasure on his face and understood why he had thanked him, even though it had nothing to do with what he had just said.

"Yes, Ludwig," Studer said, "you're going to be rich. But when you've got the money you must never forget you were once in the poorhouse. You lived in the woods with Barbara and wove baskets. Why? Just to be free. Freedom . . . Nowadays people don't know what real freedom is.

"Wait for me here," said Studer, pushing open the door leading into the hall of the horticultural college. Silence. Just the murmur of the little fountain; the chrysanthemums had a graveyard scent. No one in the long corridor. On the other side of the door opposite the principal's office a monotonous voice could be heard. Studer recognized it.

". . .thus arsenic is the basic component of a number of pesticides. It can also be found in plant disinfectants, Uspulun, for example . . ." Studer gave a sharp knock and opened the door.

Students were sitting on the benches, three rows, one higher than the other. They nodded to Studer. Then their heads bent down over their exercise books once more, fountain pens scratched. The students were taking notes.

Wottli went red. It was not a natural blush; his face was blotchy.

"Wha . . . What is it you want?"

"It will only take a moment. If you don't mind."

"Of course."

The teacher followed the sergeant out into the corridor. Studer went into the principal's office – it was empty – asked Wottli to wait outside, then shut the door and made a telephone call. The conversation took some time, but when it was over he knew that Ernst Äbi's body was to be collected in an hour. Out in the corridor he called for Ludwig Farny, handed him the key for the door to the glasshouse and told him to wait there. No one was to enter the place apart from the two officers who were coming to collect the body. And once they'd finished he was to lock the door. Had he got that?

"Yes . . . Studer."

"Good."

Wottli's self-assurance had vanished. The tall, skinny man was standing, head bowed, in the middle of the corridor, his hands clasped against his chest. The sergeant felt sorry for him – Studer had a soft heart.

Changing to a more familiar tone, he said, "First of all show me the dead man's desk. Then I'd like to go somewhere where we can talk undisturbed. Where do you suggest, Wottli? ("Wottli" without the "Herr" was an experiment. How would the teacher react to it?)

"My room, Studer, if that's all right by you?"

The sergeant was pleased; his experiment had succeeded. This bony fellow had softened – he would talk. And Studer was sure he would have plenty to tell. For a while Wottli was silent, and Studer waited patiently. Finally he spoke.

"Do you mind going to the classroom yourself, Studer? I've had enough. One of the students will show you Äbi's desk. Yes?"

Studer nodded. He was sure searching the desk was pointless, but he had to go through the motions so he could say he'd gone through the motions.

He was right. Nothing but exercise books – and they were all like the exercise books covered in oilcloth he had seen in the bright light of a lamp one July evening. Those exercise books presumably came from the same

141

shop as these. "VEGETABLES", "COMPOSTING", "GLASSHOUSE", "FRUIT TREES", etc. All in capitals. "SHRUBS". The sergeant thanked the redhead, Amstein, for his help. Then he stood in front of the blackboard like a teacher and addressed the class. He hoped, he said, the students knew what was expected of them. There was an investigation under way, and until it was completed he must ask those present not to leave the college. It was purely a matter of form, but still ... Now, he went on, he had to talk to their teacher, who was waiting outside for him, and he would ask the class to remain quiet during Herr Wottli's absence and find some other work to occupy them. Above all, he had to insist that no one enter the glass-house; it would be even better if no one went there at all. Could they promise him that? Amstein stood up and explained that he was the class representative and would make sure the sergeant's request was observed.

Studer thanked them and went out.

"Right then," said Studer once he was out in the corridor, "now we can go. Where is it you live, Wottli?"

"At the Sun Inn."

Studer stopped. "Where?" he asked in astonishment.

"In the inn. Why are you so surprised?"

"On what floor?"

"The first floor . . . above Farny's room."

"I don't believe it!"

They took the route past the poorhouse. The court-yard was silent. Old Mother Trili wasn't doing the washing, wasn't singing. And no one was shuffling across the flattened earth with a besom . . .

The sergeant followed Wottli into his room – and was not a little surprised at what he saw there. There were two suitcases on the floor. Studer picked them up –

they were packed. On the table was a brown booklet: Wottli's Swiss passport.

"You're going away?"

"Yes . . . But I wouldn't have left without speaking to you first."

"And why do you want to go away?"

"I'm afraid, Studer."

"Of me?"

A shake of the head. Silence. Studer went on the offensive.

"What was there between you and Frau Hungerlott, Wottli?"

"So you've found out about that already, have you?"

"Remember you're living in a little village. Do you imagine no one saw you?"

"Of course . . . Well . . . But my conscience is clear. It was just that she was unhappy. Her husband tormented her, and she had no one to turn to. I ran into her once – it's a long time ago now, perhaps six months – and she spoke to me. Hungerlott wasn't there, he'd gone to Bern. That was the first time we went for a walk together. Poor Anna, she'd never had much of a life. Certainly not at home. She worked in an office, and that's where she met her husband. She really married him only to get away from the town so she wouldn't have to see her father any more. But she wasn't happy here either."

Studer had sat down and now he was sitting in his favourite posture, hands clasped, forearms on his thighs.

"What did she die of?"

"I can't tell you . . . I can't tell you."

"Why?"

"Because I have no proof."

"Who did you discuss it with?"

"How do you know? How do you know I discussed Anna's death with someone?"

Even a kindly man occasionally enjoys getting his own back.

"You thought you were such an expert in criminology? You've studied books, haven't you?"

"Please, Studer, you mustn't mock me. It was a mistake to talk like that yesterday, but I was afraid . . . afraid you might . . . you might have found something."

Found? Studer thought hard. What could he have found? His face remained expressionless as he said, "Perhaps I did."

"What must you think of me?! Do you think I've behaved stupidly?"

Behaved stupidly? Studer tried a smile. Wottli flew off the handle. "There you are! You're laughing at me! Why? Because I wrote some love letters? I loved Anna. She wanted to get a divorce; we'd have got married. She said she'd hidden my letters, and now . . . now they're in the hands of the police. Who gave you the letters? If it was Ernst Äbi, then he deserved to die. Tell me, was it Ernst Äbi? Or his father? Or his mother? I never found out where Anna hid the letters. And you were in Aarbergergasse yesterday. Seeing my mother. She tried to find the letters. Tell me who gave them to you."

Studer said nothing. Inside he felt a glow of satisfaction that he had not been wrong the previous day. The Dutch student, Popingha, had indeed handed him the end of the thread with which he could unravel the tangle.

It was obvious: the letters had been in the possession of James Farny, the Chinaman. That was why the last exercise book, the one he'd been writing in, had disappeared. The exercise book and probably a folder with papers. How had the Chinaman come to get hold of the letters?

"How did Frau Hungerlott get on with her uncle?" Studer asked.

"You refuse to answer my question and you expect me to answer yours?"

"Wottli! Just think. I can't answer because I'm not sure. You could answer my questions to help me. Will you do that? If you do, I'll do everything I can to see that you can leave on Sunday. Is it a deal?"

"Not until Sunday? Why not today? Do you think I want to be present when you reveal the solution?"

Studer racked his brains. What was the best way? Should he, the simple detective sergeant, play the judge? He sat quite still, his eyes down, while Wottli paced to and fro. The silence seemed to be more than the teacher could bear; he started speaking again agitatedly:

"Hungerlott only went to Bern once a week – I could only see Anna once a week. We were so careful, we always met in the woods, we were never seen together in Pfründisberg, but one of the students caught us in the woods. Yes, caught us! It was the Dutch student, and he grinned . . . Anna only came to see me here at the inn once, she got them to call me down. Her husband wanted to have her stepbrother arrested. She liked Ludwig and asked me to speak to her husband. I did, though I wasn't happy with it. And since I couldn't see her, I wrote letters. I wrote every day while she was ill and gave them to her brother, who went to see her every day. Once – no, a few times I also asked her uncle to take them. He went to see her too. Once she gave Ernst a letter to me. In it she said someone was poisoning her, but I couldn't believe it, even though . . . even though I . . . the warden . . . No, I can't say it."

Silence. Studer waited. His chair was at the table with the passport on it. The teacher had sat down on the bed behind him. Studer listened, his leg muscles tensed – the slightest sound, and he would let himself fall to his right to evade an attack. If, however, there was no attack, then at least *one* person would have proved his innocence. To be quite sure, he asked quietly, "What was the name of the seed disinfectant, Wottli?"

A sigh. It sounded like a sigh of relief. He heard steps, firm steps, not someone creeping up behind. Wottli stood before the sergeant, ramrod straight. "So, you've understood, have you? Yesterday, when I saw the Uspulun – yes, that's the name, Uspulun – in the dead student's pocket, I knew Anna was right. She'd been poisoned by her brother. Why? Because Ernst wanted to get the inheritance. How do you think a teacher feels when he finds out that one of his students is a murderer? And the murderer commits suicide? You surely don't believe that about the key being swapped, do you?"

Studer sat there, motionless. He didn't raise his head, and he kept his hands clasped.

"When you think of the things the newcomer, his uncle, did for the lad! And I'm convinced Ernst didn't just kill his sister, he killed his uncle as well. Aren't you, Studer? Come on, say something. Don't just sit there like a statue. Farny wanted to buy a house here, and I was to design the garden, lay it out with my students. I suggested he organize a competition among the students. They were each to draw up a plan, and the winner would get five hundred francs. It was a great idea, and James (Wottli pronounced it "Djams") agreed. I didn't want anything, and when he promised me a legacy I got angry and said I'd never accept it. 'You will do when I'm dead, Paul,' he said. That's the way it was."

Studer's hands unclasped slowly, very slowly, his legs stretched, his massive, broad torso rose, his moustache quivered. His eyes went round the room, saw the books on the walls: Gross and Locard and Rhodes. They reminded him of his own library.

"Paul," said the sergeant, placing his hands on the teacher's shoulders, "you are a great detective. But do me one favour. Finish packing and get out of the country today. Go to the seaside, if you like. Send me your address when you've found somewhere to stay so I can keep you posted. It's better if you leave straight away, you understand? Without going to see your mother. Aarbergergasse's not a healthy place for you to be at the moment. Goodbye and *bon voyage*."

Studer went to the door, turned around and waved. "Goodbye," he repeated. "I'll explain your . . . your . . . absence to Sack-Amherd."

Paul Wottli, teacher of chemistry, composting, pot-plants, specialist in orchids, stood motionless in the middle of the room. He listened to the heavy tread that made the wooden stairs groan. As the sound died away, the thin man suddenly came back to life. He rushed over to the door, flung it open and leaned over the banisters.

"Studer! Studer!" No reply. Wottli sighed, then he could not repress a laugh. It was a low, quiet laugh. "I'll write to him," he whispered. "That was Studer! And he called me Paul!"

A blank day

It was already half past eleven when Studer left the inn to go and find Ludwig Farny. He was standing outside the door to the glasshouse, talking to two men. One, short and lively, was smoking a cigarette; the other, who looked like a retired champion wrestler, was sucking a cigar. They both waved when they saw Studer appear and strolled over to meet him.

"So there you are," said the sergeant. "You got here quickly. And you've already met my assistant?"

Murmann, who had given up his post as the village policeman in Gerzenstein a year ago because his wife preferred living in the city, nodded and tapped his cigar with his forefinger. Young Ludwig knew what he was doing, he said. The short, lively officer – his name was Reinhardtt – agreed.

Had the body already been collected? Studer asked. The two nodded. Murmann walked on Studer's right, Reinhardtt on his left; Ludwig Farny came and handed the sergeant the key to the glasshouse door.

"There was no one else here?" he asked. A shake of the head. "Good, then you two can have a rest today. I won't be needing you until tomorrow. You can go back to Gampligen, if you like. I presume you came on your bike, Murmann? Yes?" The ex-champion wrestler nodded.

"Stay in one of the inns in Gampligen – I think the Crown's quite good – and wait there. If I need you today, I'll give you a ring. I'm going to finish this off tomorrow. There're people coming to visit the poor-house, that'll be a good opportunity. It means we'll have an audience and witnesses. I'm looking forward to it. Is any of our lot coming?"

"The superintendent said he'd been invited. The clerk to the Poor Board's giving him a lift in his car."

"Who else's coming?"

"A few members of the Canton parliament, a secretary from the Department and two junior doctors, one from Meiringen, I don't know where the other's from."

"Mhm . . . Right, see you tomorrow."

The two policemen said goodbye.

"Come on, Ludwig, help me with the search." They went into the glasshouse, opened the door that had been locked – from inside – the previous day, and Studer slowly walked round the square table, one half of which was enclosed in six-inch planks. The soil that was piled up inside them was covered with a layer of wood shavings; it was probably intended to help stop the plants' roots from drying out.

"This is where Ernst was lying," Studer said, musing. "And that's where your stepfather was standing – or would you rather I called him Äbi?" Ludwig just nodded. "Let's search here. There's a hand fork; we can use that. Studer started to work on the wood shavings with the prongs of the fork. He worked slowly and methodically, all the time talking to Ludwig.

"Wottli brought you your supper last night. Can you remember whether Ernst drank any of the coffee?"

Ludwig looked up in surprise. "How do you know, Herr Studer?"

The sergeant paused in his work. "What did you say, Ludwig?" Ludwig blushed.

"How do you know?" A pause, then, "Studer?"

"That's better. How do I know? I'll show you when the time comes. Now let's get on with the search."

Ludwig dug his nails into the soil that had been turned over. Suddenly he said, "Here!" and held out a rusty key to the sergeant. Studer picked it up between his thumb and index finger, took it to the light and gave the end a long and reflective examination. "It's true. Come on, Ludwig."

Outside, Studer locked the door and set off for the inn. "That's one of the locales sorted out," he muttered, "now let's go and deal with the second. We'll leave the third until tomorrow."

Studer halted at the foot of the stone steps and looked across to the graveyard. Then he shrugged his shoulders. "Come on, Ludwig," he said, "we've got to get shaved. You're getting a beard."

He went into the kitchen and demanded some hot water. Huldi promised to bring a jug. Then he went to the room where, not so long ago, the Chinaman had lived.

The waitress brought the water he'd asked for, and the sergeant lathered his cheeks, then handed Ludwig the brush. "You might as well use the razor too – if you'd like."

He could tell from the look on Ludwig's face that he felt as if he had just received the accolade. To be allowed to use the same razor as the sergeant!

"*Meerci* ... Yes, I would ... Studer," the lad stammered, flushing bright red.

There was a knock at the door. "Come in," Studer wheezed as he wiped the foam out of his ears. The innkeeper appeared. "Sergeant! Wottli's gone!"

"He has, has he?" said Studer, drying his face. "Then we can go up to his room." He sat down on the bed and waited for Ludwig to finish. "I don't need you,

Brönnimann. When can we eat? Soon? Say in half an hour? I'm going to fetch a friend."

The innkeeper left, and they could hear him giving orders in the kitchen.

"Let's go, Ludwig." The two of them went up the stairs, opened the door of the empty room and went in. The books were still on the shelves that were fixed to the walls. Studer went over to them. There was a small glass tube by a fat tome. The sergeant picked it up, went over to the window and read the label. He removed the cork, shook out one of the tiny pills into the palm of his hand and murmured, "No taste, no smell. Good medicine, covered by the law on the use of narcotics, of course . . . Did you feel a bit dizzy when you woke up yesterday evening? Did you, Ludwig?"

Yes, the lad replied, he'd not felt very well.

"Poor old Wottli! He must have seen Ernst together with his father. Perhaps he suspected something. And in order to be left in peace he tried to send you both to sleep. If Ernst had drunk his coffee, he wouldn't have died."

"So you think . . . er . . . Studer, that Ernst committed suicide? Is that what Wottli told you?"

"Wottli thought so – because he didn't know we've found the key. Go down to the bar and wait for me there. I'm going to fetch the lawyer."

"Which lawyer?"

"You slept well last night." Studer laughed, went to the door, then stopped. "We've finished with the second locale now. How will we get on with the third?"

Fifteen minutes later Studer returned. With a black look on his face. He seemed not to notice Ludwig, went straight to the telephone, dialled a number, asked to speak to Reinhardt of the Cantonal Police and waited. Then: "You're both to come back here. Leave the bike a couple of hundred yards before the inn. Then search the woods. Münch has disappeared. They told me they'd seen him set off for his office in Bern, but I know that's not true. I interrogated the warder in the poorhouse and a few of the inmates. No one saw Münch this morning, and Hungerlott claims he left at eight. There's something wrong there."

The sergeant was proved right. He sat in the bar the whole afternoon. At six the telephone rang. Since there was no one in the room apart from himself and Ludwig, he answered it himself. Murmann spoke – Studer nodded. Then the sergeant said quietly, "Let Reinhardt go back on foot, and you take the injured man on your bike. Look after him and bring him here tomorrow morning."

That night Studer's sleep was deep and untroubled. But Ludwig sat there in the dark watching over the friend who was like a father to him.

The beginning of an end

At half past five a car drove up outside, and Studer woke up. He put his coat on, crept down to the front door and slid the bolt back. He saw three people get out of the car, then it drove off. They made their way to the steps slowly, the one in the middle leaning heavily on the other two.

"Morning, Hans," said Studer softly.

"*Salut.*" Münch smiled.

"Come along. You can have a lie down on my bed. And don't talk too much. You can tell us your story after lunch. I don't think they know yet over there. Yesterday Hungerlott invited me to lunch."

"You watch out, Studer," Münch mumbled. He had difficulty in speaking. "You don't realize what a risk you're taking. They're devious . . . Have you still got the letter and the will?"

They were back in Studer's room. Münch lay down. At eight Studer sent Ludwig to fetch some breakfast. "You bring it up yourself," he ordered.

Until eleven o'clock the three of them held a council of war. Then, once Studer had revealed everything he knew, he stood up. Cars were driving past outside. The visitors to the poorhouse were beginning to arrive.

"You're coming with me, Ludwig," the sergeant commanded. The two of them set off. They went into the poorhouse – the hall was empty. Studer pushed open the door to the inmates' refectory. The tables were all occupied, the inmates had freshly washed blue overalls, there was the smell of a meaty broth. The bowls were full to the brim, and everyone had half a loaf of bread. The inmates were eating.

Studer asked to be taken to the warden. This time the warder accompanied them, but he did not pull the bell. He bent down, low and obsequiously, until he was level with the doorknob, listened at the keyhole, then knocked softly. Inside a conversation stopped. The door was flung open, and Vinzenz Hungerlott exclaimed delightedly, "Ah! The sergeant."

Studer must come in, he went on, he would meet some old friends. Only then did the warden notice Ludwig Farny, and he pulled a face as if he had toothache. That man had not been invited, he said, did he have to come?

"Yes," said Studer curtly.

Hungerlott pretended he hadn't noticed Studer's impoliteness. His gesture of invitation could have been directed at both of them – or only the sergeant. Studer sneaked a look at his companion. Strange, the lad had not blushed.

The two of then went in, along a corridor. A maid opened a door into a room where the air was blue with cigar smoke. There were liqueur glasses everywhere.

"Elsi! Two more glasses," Herr Hungerlott ordered.

The introductions did not take long. Most of the men there knew Studer – he had once been an inspector with the Bern City Police. Two clerks from the Poor Board – both puffed up with pride when they were addressed as "*Herr Sekretär*" – an elderly man from the Society for the Welfare of Released Prisoners who was hard of hearing, members of parliament in cutaway coats. And there was another man there, sitting somewhat apart from the others: the chief superintendent, Studer's boss. He had a pale complexion and a long, grey moustache. "Aha, Studer." The well-dressed gentleman nodded and waved his skinny hand. "Well then? Have you discovered anything?"

"I think we should wait until after lunch," Studer whispered.

"All right, if you think so – but don't make a fool of yourself."

Studer shook his head. "Not today," he whispered, "definitely not today. I won't be able to explain everything, but I've invited two other people, a man and a woman. They'll come after lunch."

Studer looked across at Hungerlott. The warden was engrossed in a conversation with one of the junior doctors. Arnold Äbi was sitting next to him, not looking particularly out of place.

"What's that cop doing here?" one of the clerks bellowed. Studer blinked and said that the deputy governor from Roggwil had called him in, and since the matter had been sorted out, he'd accepted an invitation to a good lunch. His last words were drowned out in a gale of laughter – one of the members of parliament had told a joke. Someone else started to tell one . . . more laughter . . . Hungerlott filled the glasses . . . toasts were drunk . . . the blue smoke got thicker.

Studer stood by the window, looking out over the countryside and wondering why the whole gathering seemed unreal to him: the clinking of glasses, the aperitifs, the laughter at the jokes, the aroma of the expensive cigars, the cigarettes. Out of the window the sergeant could see the graveyard on the right with its memorials of red and white stone, its black wooden crosses – and its fresh graves. Immediately in front of him was the Sun Inn and on the left, about four hundred yards away stood – broad, massive and white, only the roof had black tiles – the horticultural college. The ground-floor windows were open, framing young heads whose eyes were presumably fixed on the glass cube of the hothouse, where one of them had died the previous evening.

Studer felt troubled, but not by the view of the two locales he had finished with, nor by the sight of all the fruit trees, which, correctly pruned according to the Pfründisberg method, looked slightly deformed. No, what he found depressing, eerie even, was what was going on behind his back. A murderer, perhaps even two were putting on a show of innocence to win the last round. Had they trumps up their sleeves? Were they going to try something on? Did they think they were safe because of what they'd done the previous day to try to silence the most dangerous witness, Münch, the lawyer? And what was the threat to him, the detective who was on the spot, whose character reference was poor and friends few and far between?

Behind him a voice said, "They take themselves far too seriously, the cops. Far too seriously."

"Just what I think," said another voice in a thick Swiss accent. The sergeant thought he recognized the voice. He turned his head a little and squinted out of the corner of his eye. Of course! Arnold Äbi had to have his say. He was sitting by the stove in his dark, well-brushed Sunday suit, nodding from time to time, saying the odd word to agree with what someone else had said; in short, he was being careful not to draw attention to himself, he didn't even dare cross his legs.

As Studer was glancing round the room, another face caught his eye. Ludwig Farny was sitting, silent, in one corner. He had his right leg crossed over his left, and his hands clasped round his knees. His cheap suit had also been brushed clean – Huldi had probably helped him there. His fixed expression looked almost

156

arrogant and his eyes, which had that striking blue gleam, were fastened on his stepfather. There was contempt in them and pride. And did Ludwig Farny not have good reason to be proud? Had he not discovered from the policemen's discussions that he would inherit James Farny's fortune along with his mother? That the two men who had tormented him – one while he was a little boy, the other later on – would not only end up empty-handed, they would end up in a cell, on thin soup and chicory coffee?

He raised his eyes, fixed them on the massive figure of the sergeant, then higher . . . The two men nodded imperceptibly as another burst of laughter rang out. None of the others present had noticed the mute agreement between the two.

Vinzenz Hungerlott was wearing a black frock coat and a clip-on cravat; his tiepin had an artificial pearl, which gleamed briefly when his beard jutted out horizontally. A knock at the door, the warden raised his hands for silence: "Lunch is served, gentlemen." They made their way in good order, thin, transparent ribbons rising up to the ceiling from many of the ashtrays. They went along a corridor with red stoneware tiles (gleaming from the application of floor polish) until the maid opened a door: "If you would be so good . . ."

The long table was covered with a damask cloth; at every setting a variety of crystal glasses twinkled. (Studer recalled the glasses that had appeared in The Sun one July evening: relics, presumably, of the time when the inn had been part of a spa.) When the guests were seated, the girl started ladling out soup on the sideboard, filling one plate at a time and bringing it to the table. Now there was a clatter of spoons on the china soup-plates and the sound of slurping. "An exquisite soup!" – "Excellent!" – "He can afford a good cook." Hungerlott nodded his thanks and stroked his goatee.

At the bottom of the table, where the unimportant guests are usually seated, were Studer and Ludwig Farny. The sergeant marvelled at the dainty way Ludwig handled his spoon. And he didn't slurp his soup – higher up the table things were much noisier.

An interrupted lunch

"Well, Sergeant, aren't you going to tell us some of your experiences with the police? That business with the bank, for example? You were an inspector with the City Police at the time, weren't you, and you didn't need to go looking among ex-inmates of the poorhouse for your friends?" The speaker seemed flattered by the laughter that followed – Hungerlott bowed his head like an actor receiving applause.

Ludwig Farny started and opened his mouth, but Studer kicked him on the ankle. "Keep calm, lad," he whispered, then cleared his throat.

"Yes, at the time I wasn't interested in pauperism," he said dryly. "To find out about pauperism, you have to have lunch with a poorhouse warden."

Shocked silence. The maid began to clear away the plates, and her sharp elbow caught Studer on the side of the head. The sergeant looked up. The girl had green eyes, and they were filled with hatred. "Mm," Studer muttered. Münch was right, he'd better watch out. Since the silence continued, Studer went on, "I do have another friend, besides Ludwig, and I'm worried about him. I had hoped to find him here. Could you tell me where Herr Münch is, Herr Hungerlott?"

The warden really was a good actor. His eyebrows went up in an expression of astonishment. "But I told you yesterday that Herr Münch went back to Bern in the morning."

"Strange. I couldn't contact him either at home or in his office."

"Then it would have made more sense for you to go back to town, wouldn't it?"

Studer said nothing. The chief superintendent started to speak, thus ending the first preliminary skirmish.

The maid poured red wine from a dusty bottle, making sure the sergeant and his protégé were the last to be served. Then a warmed plate was set before each of the guests, and a tray handed round with veal vol-au-vents. This time as well, the pair at the bottom were the last to be served.

Had Reinhardt, had Murmann managed to get into the poorhouse unobserved and search the warden's study? Or had Hungerlott countered that move by placing the inmates, who had made a racket in the inn the previous evening – Studer was sure he'd seen the same faces on 18 July – as sentries in the corridors?

"Don't drink the wine," Studer whispered. Hungerlott seemed to have heard his warning, however, for he stood up and went round the table, clinking glasses with everyone – and each of the guests emptied his glass. The sergeant took a sip and put his glass down; Ludwig followed his example. With concern in his voice, the warden enquired if Studer was ill? And Arnold Äbi asked his stepson what was wrong? It was good wine. Ludwig did not reply.

"That's the way things are," old Äbi moaned. "You do everything you can to bring up your children, give them a good education – and when you take them out into polite society, they show you up."

"Shhh!" Studer whispered to his assistant, who was about to protest vigorously that Äbi wasn't his father. It was a tense situation. Of course, there was no risk for

160

the gentlemen who just wanted to have a look at a poorhouse to pass the time, but there was danger for a simple detective, when the murderer knew he didn't believe in gastric influenza. Gastric influenza could be highly infectious if you didn't know how many of the pellets, which a German chemical factory had sent to a horticultural college for testing, had disappeared. Those pellets dissolved quite easily – and you had to take into account that your host was a widower, that the widower had a maidservant, and that a widower was a desirable catch. To become the warden's wife, a girl like that would carry out all kinds of orders, orders that could be easily explained away: it was just a joke; they wanted to play a trick on a smart-ass cop, give him a laxative – no harm done, but amusing for the other guests. Wouldn't he look a fool! And once the detective had swallowed the dissolved pellet and felt ill, it would be easy, under the pretence of coming to his assistance, to get hold of his wallet and with it the documents. Who else would the lawyer have given them to? With a lethargic look on his face, Studer made a request. Would Herr Hungerlott allow him to make a quick telephone call? Perhaps Münch had got home by now. There was something he had to tell him. (It was, of course, a pretext, Studer just wanted to see if the two detectives were searching the warden's study.)

When Studer's face had the expression of a ruminating ox, he was usually paying close attention. So he did not miss the exchange of glances between Hungerlott and Äbi. Fear? Uncertainty? No, hostility. Had the two of them fallen out? It was a possibility. When money's at stake, friendship often goes by the board.

The warden forced himself to smile. Of course, he was happy to put the telephone at the sergeant's disposal.

161

"Come on, Ludwig." Studer stood up. He was more and more impressed by his assistant's rapid grasp of the situation. He calmly wiped his lips with his serviette, put it down on the table and followed his friend.

As Studer closed the door behind him, more laughter burst out in the room. The sergeant quickly found his bearings: that was the door to the study. He opened it – it was empty.

What now? Where were Reinhardt and Murmann? What had delayed them? The sergeant tried to open the desk drawers – they were all locked. He picked up the folder lying on the desk – it was empty apart from a few sheets of blotting paper.

"Have a quick look behind the books, Ludwig," the sergeant whispered, opening the door into a neighbouring room. There were two beds in it, fine redwood furniture. One was by the window, the other along the back wall. The sergeant guessed that in the past they had been next to each other. The room had three doors: the one Studer had come in by, one opposite leading into another room and the third, which presumably led out into the corridor. The second room would be the one where Münch had slept. Hungerlott and his father-in-law had been sitting in the study, and the lawyer had been able to slip out through the third door. Studer went back into the study.

"Found anything, Ludwig?"

"Only this exercise book."

A book with oilcloth covers . . . A diary . . . Presumably James Farny's handwriting. The last entry was dated 17.XI. Damn! He was out of luck. James Farny had written in English, and his handwriting was not easy to decipher. But he had filled four pages, and the end looked bizarre: a blot and a hole in the paper. Had

162

his fountain pen broken? Studer tore the leaves out of the book. "Put it back, Ludwig. Where was it?"

"Behind those books there."

Studer went over, and while Ludwig was replacing the exercise book, he read the titles. Detective novels seemed popular in Pfründisberg. It wasn't only Wottli who had that kind of book on his shelves. Agatha Christie, Edgar Wallace . . . Studer remembered that he had noticed them before. When Münch had been sitting in an armchair by the fire.

Footsteps approached, the door opened. Hungerlott came in.

"Finished, Sergeant?"

"Yes, *meerci*. I managed to have a word with Münch."

"You did? Really? That's strange . . ." Studer grinned inwardly, but then immediately gave himself a mental slap on the wrist when the warden went on, "Strange, yes. The maid didn't hear you making your call. But come and join us again. And you there too." Ludwig bared his teeth like an angry dog, but the sergeant patted him on the shoulder. "Go and get me something from the inn. All right? Off you go." Ludwig understood. He was to look for Reinhardt and Murmann.

And its continuation

The two sheets of paper were in Studer's breast pocket. He followed the warden back to the lunch table. There was a smell of roast meat and insipid mashed potatoes; the salad had been supplied by the college. The red-wine glasses were empty – apart from Studer's and Ludwig's – and the maid was going round with a long-necked bottle serving white wine. This time the warden only clinked glasses with the man beside him, the police superintendent. Both took a sip and smacked their lips as they savoured the wine. "La Neuveville 1928," said the superintendent. Flattered, the warden nodded. "You're a connoisseur, Warden."

Studer felt as if he were in a dream. There had been too many new impressions, one after the other: too many new locales to get to know. He saw the men sitting round the table, and at the same time he saw Ernst Äbi lying dead in the glasshouse of the horticultural college.

As if in a dream . . .

There had been an orchid in flower in the glass-house and, strangely, the sergeant could see the flower quite clearly. It was shaped like a human face – no, more like a mask, but that wasn't quite right either. It was like a wax head – but that was wrong too. With its background of soil and moss it was like the face of the dead Chinaman, for that had also lain on soil and moss.

Äbi asked in malevolent tones, "Well then, Sergeant Studer, what have you done with your protégé?"

A scathing reply was on the tip of Studer's tongue, but he repressed it and replied calmly, "He's gone to do an errand for me."

He stretched out his hand, as if to pick up his wine glass, then drew his hand back – the glass shattered on the floor. He apologized volubly. He was truly sorry. To be so clumsy! When he looked up he saw Hungerlott's furrowed brow. The warden emptied his glass, waved the maid over, got her to fill it and emptied it again. The beads of sweat stood out on Äbi's forehead.

The half-deaf welfare official rose, wiped his lips, cleared his throat and started to make a speech. He praised the good administration of the poorhouse, offered the warden his condolences for his sad loss . . . But once again, he went on, one could see that a true man did not let himself be ground down by fate. The warden was still carrying out his difficult task, was getting those in his charge to do useful work, was transforming wasted lives into workers serving the nation. In brief, here was a man who could serve as a model for the younger generation. His devotion to duty showed how one could overcome personal sorrow. He raised his glass to a man who had performed outstanding services for the state. That was all he had to say.

Chairs were pushed back. The maid filled the glasses with Schaffis wine. The guests surrounded Hungerlott, drank to him, showered praise, condolences on him. Their voices were slightly slurred; their faces had a bluish tinge.

"We'll have coffee in my study," Hungerlott said. "If you would follow me, gentlemen." He led the way.

Studer felt uncomfortable. If Murmann and his lively colleague Reinhardt were searching the study at that very moment, then there was a public outcry in store for him. Therefore the sergeant hung behind and waited until the warden had opened the door to his study. When he heard no outraged exclamations he joined the back of the group.

The large coffee machine was plugged in, and the brown liquid was bubbling under the glass lid. Finally the warden took the plug out, the bubbling died down, the cups were filled. Each time one of the visitors took his cup, Hungerlott asked, "Kirsch? Rum? Plum brandy?" Soon all the little glasses beside the coffee cups were filled. Some of the gentlemen tossed them back, others sucked up the strong liqueur in tiny sips, fat cigars were lit. Studer, who had not been offered a cigar, made do with one of his Brissagos.

The police superintendent began to tease his subordinate. What kind of a murder was it? Had Köbu got a bee in his bonnet again? Without wanting to suggest anything untoward – he smiled at the warden – could it not be a simple love story: a middle-aged man had fallen in love with his niece and couldn't come to terms with her death? Suicide? Eh? As far as he was aware, the local doctor supported the suicide theory, and it was only a young deputy governor, who was keen to make his mark, who thought it was murder.

When Studer replied it was in High German. "It is of course possible that I've got a bee in my bonnet. But in that case, perhaps you would be so good as to explain how a man who has shot himself in the heart can put on a clean shirt and button up his waistcoat, jacket and coat? If you can explain those anomalies, then I'll be happy to accept the suicide theory."

Silence. People always felt uncomfortable when Studer spoke High German. In the first place he articulated the words perfectly, not like a Bernese with his thick gutturals; and then, as all the gentlemen agreed, this sergeant would not stand any nonsense.

After all, they had come to enjoy a pleasant lunch, not to hear a detective's report about a case of murder. The superintendent put on a look of annoyance, but Studer continued.

"I'd very much like to hear what you think about gastric influenza, Chief Superintendent."

"Gastric influenza?" his boss asked. His face was covered in a network of fine wrinkles.

"Yes, gastric influenza," said Studer in a matter-of-fact voice. "The day before yesterday I discovered by chance" – he stressed the words "by chance" – "three ladies' handkerchiefs, which I took to the Institute for Forensic Medicine. The analysis carried out by the doctor there showed beyond any shadow of doubt that the mucus on the handkerchiefs contained arsenic ..." Studer's gaze went round the room, and he saw that all the men were looking at him; turning to them, he said dryly, "Perhaps you gentlemen know that arsenic is a poison?"

That was too much! Should they sit there and let themselves be made fun of by a simple detective sergeant? The air hummed with guttural Swiss outrage: "*Chabis!* Rubbish!" – "Pure fabrication!" – Prove it! Prove your allegation!" Studer raised his hand to calm the hubbub. As he did so, he recalled the scene with which it had all begun: the local doctor, Dr Buff, arguing with Ochsenbein, the deputy governor, by the body of the Chinaman ...

A sharp voice asked, "Are you accusing me, Sergeant?" Hungerlott was sitting up stiffly in his chair – and the man was very pale.

"I? Accuse you? Why ever should I do that?" It was clear that the formal German of the discussion was getting on the guests' nerves. "How could I accuse you? I have no proof."

The warden leaned back, crossed his legs, dipped a lump of sugar in his kirsch, popped it in his mouth and emptied his liqueur glass. As he crunched up the sugar, he said, his mouth full, "I suggest we call an end to the discussion of this unpleasant topic and start our tour of the poorhouse. Sergeant Studer can accompany us, should he so desire . . ." Although his mouth was full of sugar, the last words sounded bitter.

"Of course." – "Let's get on with it." – "We want to see the place." Studer stayed at the back. He had an uneasy feeling. The search of the study obviously hadn't worked. Why had Reinhardt and Murmann not come?

With dignified steps, the warden led the way.

"We insist on cleanliness above all else. Cleanliness is our best weapon against pauperism. Cleanliness and a healthy diet. Before I take you to the dormitories, I will show you gentlemen the kitchen. You can try the soup the inmates had today."

A huge stove . . . pans on it. There were two men in the kitchen; they were wearing clean white aprons and flat white caps.

"Our cooks are also residents here, our bakers too. – Moser, ladle out a plate of soup so the gentlemen can taste it." The tin bowl had been cleaned with sandpaper. There were blobs of fat floating on the top of the thick pea soup.

"Wonderful," said one of the clerks in a deep bass voice as he tried the soup. "I'd be glad if my wife made me soup like that every day."

"Wouldn't you like a taste, Sergeant?" the warden asked with a smile. Studer declined the offer.

He was thinking of the schnapps the inmates went to fetch on a Saturday evening with the one franc they'd earned for a week's work. He felt sick.

168

They left the kitchen.

"Now," said Hungerlott, "I'll show you our residents' dormitories, then, if you are agreeable, we can see the workshops, the market garden, the farm . . ."

None of the visitors heard the remark of one of the cooks, only Studer caught it because he was the last to leave; "All lies . . ." It wouldn't be so bad if it wasn't for all the damn lies. After all, it was bearable in the kitchen, but for the others who had to slave away all morning on a billycan of thin coffee and three potatoes, for them it was hard.

The courtyard was empty, there was a cold north wind blowing. In one corner old Mother Trili was standing at her tub and washing, washing, washing . . . Her lips were cracked, and she wasn't singing; from time to time a nasty cough tore at her chest. When she saw the sergeant, she waved to him and when he was closer, she asked, "What did you do with my Hansli?"

Studer shrugged his shoulders, he felt a lump in his throat which made it impossible to speak.

In an open shed four old men were chopping up firewood.

"The antidote to pauperism," Hungerlott was saying in his pontificating manner, "is work, work, work. Anyone who does not work has no right to eat. Even for the oldest, even for the weakest I can always find some task they are capable of carrying out. In that way they do not feel useless, they feel they have earned their food, that their pocket money is a wage and not charity.

"I would like to thank the Poor Board for the understanding they have always shown; it is their understanding that has made it possible for me to carry out this difficult task to the best of my knowledge and ability and help many a lost soul back onto the rails. I know that there are those who begrudge me my success (a venomous glance at the sergeant), but despite all aspersions cast at me, I do my duty and . . ."

Hungerlott fell silent and looked at the gate into the courtyard. The visitors, who had listened to his speech with their hands clasped over their bellies – and smouldering cigars in the corner of their mouths – rubbed their eyes as they too looked towards the gate . . .

A lawyer appears

His right arm round Ludwig's shoulder, his left round Reinhardt's, Münch staggered in through the gate. His coat was torn, there was a bruise on his forehead, and two bloodstained handkerchiefs were tied round his neck. Studer went up to him.

"*Salut*, Münch," he said calmly.

"*Salut*, Studer," was the hoarse reply.

"Don't you want to take your coat off?" the sergeant asked.

The lawyer shook his head wearily. He could see the chief superintendent of the Cantonal Police over there, he said, that was presumably the right man to make a statement to.

"But not here," Studer said, "we must get you somewhere warm."

Münch nodded.

Studer suddenly heard a well-known voice behind him shouting, "Stop!" When he turned around, he had to smile. The scene he saw was so much like something out of an American gangster film that he couldn't take it seriously. Murmann had a revolver in his hand and was not letting old Äbi out of his sight.

"Should I handcuff him, Sergeant?" he asked.

In a shrill voice Hungerlott said, "I protest. This is not the way judicial proceedings should be carried out. A detective sergeant and a superintendent are not authorized to take statements – I mean statements that are valid in court . . ."

But who was that coming through the gate? Elegant in his waspwaisted coat? Herr Ochsenbein, the deputy governor, followed by an officer of the rural gendarmerie in uniform. The hilt of the policeman's sabre had been polished until it shone.

"What's . . . all . . . this?"

"You got someone to telephone me, Sergeant?" Ochsenbein asked. He raised his bowler hat and saluted the assembled crowd.

"I repeat my previous suggestion," Studer said, "Let's go back to Herr Hungerlott's study and, if you gentlemen will allow me, I will tell you a story. I do not require any statements. Murmann, you keep your eye on Äbi."

Again Studer let the others go on ahead. Immediately in front of him Detective Constable Murmann strode along majestically. Studer brought up the rear, Ludwig Farny sticking by his side.

At first there was chaos. Chairs had to be brought in, and it was some time before all the officials were seated. Münch had been given the most comfortable armchair; a stool was put in front of it, cushions laid on top, and his legs carefully placed on them. It had to be admitted that Münch looked rather dazed.

Studer said, "Tell us what happened, Münch. I know, but now you must inform the others."

And the lawyer started. His expression livened up. He began by talking about his acquaintance with the remarkable expatriate Swiss, about the will he had made. Even then, he said, the Chinaman (the nickname came from his friend, Studer) had feared he might be murdered. Not that the man was afraid, on the contrary. He was brave. Only he didn't want his wealth to fall into the hands of people who didn't deserve it. If he had died without making a will, it would have gone to his family. Farny had had nothing against his relatives, but both his sister and his niece were married – and he didn't like either of their husbands.

"Just a moment, Münch," Studer interrupted. "It would be a good idea if we searched one of those husbands. Off you go, Reinhardt."

Äbi resisted, but it was no use. Studer didn't even need to intervene. The man had a small gun in his back trouser pocket. The sergeant took it. "A 6.35." He nodded. Then he flicked open the butt. Two bullets were missing in the magazine. When he pulled the slide back an unused cartridge fell out. "So one bullet has been fired," Studer said, without looking up. "Continue, Münch."

"Eventually one of the husbands managed to ingratiate himself. When his wife died, he persuaded my client to bequeath him the portion that would have gone to his wife. But James Farny inserted in his will the condition that the widower must pass on half of his share to a friend of his. He intended to keep it a secret, but he liked talking, did James Farny. One evening he told the friend concerned, probably across there in the bar of the inn. The innkeeper overheard and passed the news on to the widower. We assume the widower kicked up a fuss – he was probably furious he would lose the money after he had committed a crime to get it. And, we assume, James Farny saw through him. Once more he feared for his life. Therefore he wrote to me and made an appointment for 18 November, at ten in the morning. When I got to Pfründisberg, James Farny was dead. Shortly after my arrival a detective turned up. I kept out of his way because I suddenly had the feeling that the death of my client was connected with the death of his niece. Therefore I went to see the widower, got him to invite me to stay. And during the very first night I had proof that I was on the right track. Someone slipped into my room and searched my clothes. Fortunately, I had hidden my wallet under my pillow. The man did not let me out of his sight the whole of the following day, but that night I managed to get out and see my friend Studer. I discussed the whole affair with him, and we came to a decision. But I didn't get back to my room. As I went out into the street a sack was thrown over my head, a couple of men grabbed me, tied me up, and I was hit over the head. When I woke up it was midday and I was at the bottom of a quarry. Those two policemen over there found me."

"That's got nothing to do with the case," said Studer. "This attack shows just one thing: someone wanted to get hold of James Farny's will. Now it's *my* turn. When, four months ago, I happened by chance to spend an evening in the Sun Inn because I'd forgotten to fill up and didn't want to push my motorbike all the way to Gampligen – after all, it was four miles and a hot summer's night with a thunderstorm threatening – I went into the innkeeper's private room, where four men were seated round a table playing *Jass*. I immediately sensed that my presence was unwelcome and asked the way out onto the terrace. I leaned on the balustrade; close in front of me was a maple, the leaves so clear I could almost could count each one. Something must have been illuminating the tree and when I looked for the source of light, I saw a brightly lit room with a man furiously writing in an exercise book. There was a pile of five other exercise books by his right elbow. I watched the man and then, unfortunately, I sneezed. The stranger leaped up, knocking his chair over; with three sideways steps he was at the window and I was *convinced* that his right hand, which was in the pocket of his camelhair smoking jacket, was holding a revolver aimed at my stomach . . . Three remarkable facts, you will agree: a stranger writing his memoirs in a rundown inn, he's armed and ready to shoot a the slightest noise. I made the stranger's acquaintance. His passport, which had been renewed in all parts of the world, in Asia, in America, was issued to a James Farny, born 13 March 1878, place of origin Gampligen, Bern Canton . . . The man flung open the window, I had to show him my identification, and it was only when Farny realized he was dealing with a police sergeant that he put his revolver away, a Colt, a large-calibre gun. Even then, four months ago, the stranger told me his life was in danger; he hoped, he said, I would be in charge of the investigation into his murder. Naturally my first thought was that I was dealing with a paranoiac, and I wondered if I should alert the medical authorities to have the man put away. Another thing I found odd was that this stranger absolutely insisted we go straight onto first name terms and use the familiar *Du* – which I, of course, refused to go along with. We went to the bar, where I got caught up in an argument. The inmates of the poorhouse, who were drinking their cheap schnapps there, and a few of the students from the horticultural college threatened to attack me, but then gave up the idea. This James Farny seemed to have some power over those who were there. Eventually the principal of the college and the warden of the poorhouse appeared (they were playing cards in the room I went into first), calmed things down and sent the students and the inmates of the poorhouse off to their beds. Brönnimann, the innkeeper, discovered a gallon can of petrol; I filled my tank and rode off. I forgot the strange scenes here until, four months later to the day, on 18 November, I was asked by the deputy governor, Herr Ochsenbein, to investigate a mysterious murder that had occurred in the graveyard in Pfründisberg . . .

"On a fresh mound over the grave where Frau Hungerlott-Äbi was buried lay the body of James Farny, whom I, because of his slit eyes, always thought of as the Chinaman. He had been killed by a shot to the heart, but neither his shirt nor his other clothes showed bloodstains. I deduced from this that he had been killed elsewhere, the body dressed and brought to the graveyard. It was important for me to determine whom the dead man had been afraid of. Since I knew from his passport that he came from Gampligen, the first suspects – once I had established that he was rich – were his relatives.

"The dead man had a married sister in Bern. Before her marriage to Arnold Äbi she had had an illegitimate son, who had been given his mother's name. He's sitting here next to me – Ludwig Farny. Farny's sister had two children by her husband: a girl, Anna, who later married Herr Hungerlott, and a son, Ernst, who was doing the one-year course at Pfründisberg Horticultural College.

"The lawyer had been asked to come and see James Farny at ten o'clock on 18 November. By then, however, the Chinaman was dead, shot through the heart. The bullet that caused his death has been lost – all that I have is the cartridge case, which I found the day before yesterday.

"Gentlemen, Anna Hungerlott-Äbi, the niece of the Chinaman, died of gastric influenza two weeks ago. Her sudden death aroused her uncle's suspicion, and that was the reason why he asked his lawyer to come and see him in Pfründisberg. Clearly, James Farny suspected Anna's husband, Herr Hungerlott, of having poisoned his wife with arsenic. Herr Münch has almost proved that.

"By chance I managed to find proof of what my friend – I think I can call him that – suspected. Three handkerchiefs that had been used by Frau Hungerlott-Äbi contained clear traces of arsenic. Dr Malapelle of the Institute for Forensic Medicine will submit a report on the matter to the relevant authorities.

"Herr Hungerlott, warden of the Pfründisberg poorhouse attempted to gain possession of the document that brought Herr Münch to Pfründisberg. My friend, Herr Münch the lawyer, also had a handwritten will drawn up by the murdered man.

"It was merely a matter of chance that Herr Hungerlott did not succeed in getting hold of these two documents. He invited the lawyer to stay in his apartment in the poorhouse. Herr Münch told you what happened during his first night there.

"There was, however, an accessory to the murder of James Farny. You will have to admit, gentlemen, that it was impossible for one person to shoot him, dress the body and take it to a place that was supposed to put the police on the wrong track. This accessory, his accomplice, was Ernst Äbi, a student at the horticultural college. It would never have occurred to me to suspect the lad. But the first day I was here a lead ball was shot through the widow of my room with a catapult. Fixed to the ball was a warning: 'Keep your fingers off our *rösti*!' It was typed, and it made me think. Warnings are not usually written in such colloquial terms, and especially not in dialect.

"The warning could not come from his father, Arnold Äbi. I knew that he was in Bern where he worked as a labourer for a coal merchant. My deduction? It must have been the man who had helped transport the body who had sent me the warning. You will ask why I did not suspect Ludwig Farny. At the time when I received the warning, Ludwig Farny was lying down in the room of Hulda Nüesch, the waitress. When, later on, I showed him the scrap of paper with the warning, he blushed, so he must have known the man who sent me the warning. Whom did Ludwig know, apart from the inmates of the poorhouse who, like all alcoholics, had loose tongues and were therefore unsuitable as accomplices? His stepbrother, Ernst Äbi. Later I learned that Ernst Äbi had helped Ludwig when he was in difficulty. At this point in the case it became clear to me that the man behind the murders might attempt to get his accomplice out of the way. That was why I gave Ludwig Farny the task of keeping an eye on his stepbrother. For I was certain, gentlemen, that Ernst Äbi would do everything to cover for his father. In the meantime I had been to Bern and had got to know, if indirectly, what kind of person Arnold Äbi was. He had money, he drank, he beat his wife and, what was the most remarkable aspect, he was a close friend of the warden of the poorhouse, Herr Hungerlott.

"It remains to be established whether this friendship dates from the time when Hungerlott married Äbi's daughter, or whether Hungerlott already knew Äbi before then. To cut a long story short, Herr Hungerlott took his friend Äbi with him to Pfründisberg. There's a second question that remains to be established: was it Hungerlott or Äbi who lured Ernst to the glasshouse that was filled with poisonous fumes?

"Ernst Äbi managed to get out of the sickbay while Ludwig Farny was asleep. He went to the prearranged meeting, which was presumably in the passage outside the glasshouses. A door's quickly opened, the lad pushed inside, the key turned in the lock from outside with a pair of pliers, *et le tour est joué* as our French neighbours say. Hungerlott probably arranged for some of the inmates of the poorhouse to kick up a racket in The Sun that would attract the students to the inn and prevent Ernst Äbi being found too soon.

"Unfortunately, Ludwig Farny woke up too late. He came to fetch me. Wottli gave me his key – we'd already ventilated the glasshouse – and we opened the door that was locked from the inside.

"Here the murderer made a mistake . . . though actually he had no choice. Either he had to let us find the key with the scratches on the metal at the end, or he had to insert another key in the lock. He probably did not have enough time to oxidise the new key to make it look like the old one. If he had done that, I wouldn't have been able to get onto the murderer. As it was, he slipped up, and that allowed me to unravel the case. Here's the key in question.

"It wasn't that slip alone that helped. In the will that James Farny left behind it specifically stated that the men, the husbands of his relatives (his sister and his niece), were not to inherit their portions. A codicil changed some things, but not much. If that will were to disappear, then Herr Hungerlott would inherit, presumably through his wife's will.

"The way the case looks to me at the moment, I have the feeling a trap was laid for my friend Münch. The only reason Arnold Äbi was brought to Pfründisberg and given a room in the warden's apartment was to get Münch to leave the building in order to see me. They probably intended to knock him down before he got to me and take the will and James Farny's letter from him."

That was the moment when Hungerlott broke in. "I would like to ask the deputy governor how long he is going to allow his subordinate to go on telling his tall stories? In Bern Sergeant Studer's imagination is notorious. From a simple policeman to the chief superintendent, they all say, 'Köbu's got another bee in his bonnet.' Isn't that right?" Studer simply stood in front of the fireplace, massive and calm, legs apart. He shrugged his shoulders.

Silence . . . an embarrassed silence. The superintendent had gone red in the face; the faces of the other visitors too recalled the colour of ripe tomatoes.

Studer turned to Arnold Äbi:

"A motorbike, a Harley-Davidson, has been registered in your name. Can you tell me where you got the money for such an expensive machine? Who paid your road tax?"

"From . . . my . . . savings," Äbi stammered.

"Reinhardt," said Studer, "bring in the woman."

The mother

Reinhardt went to the door, opened it, went out and closed it behind him. When he came back he was followed by an old woman, with short, untidy grey hair sticking out from her head. Her face was wrinkled. She was wearing a simple hat and a scarf crossed over her breast and tied at the back.

"Frau Äbi," said Studer gently, "since when has your husband had a motorbike?"

"His friend gave it to him . . ."

"Which friend?"

"Er, Hungerlott."

"When?"

"Six months ago."

"Did your husband make much use of the bike? And someone bring a chair for her."

None of the gentlemen stirred, but Ludwig Farny said, "Here you are, Mother." He went over to the old woman, took her by the arm and led her to a chair. Then he went back to stand beside his friend, Sergeant Studer.

The woman spoke. Her husband had often gone off during the night, where to she couldn't say. When they had come in the police car to collect her that morning, she had no idea what they wanted . . . She broke off to ask Ludwig how he was. Her son nodded. He was fine, he said, he'd had some good fortune and they'd probably both be rich now.

Again Hungerlott's shrill voice broke in. The civil

181

court would certainly have something to say about getting rich. The maid with the white apron and the white cap on her bobbed hair came in bearing a tray full of clinking glasses. In her right hand she was carrying three bottles by the neck. The warden said he presumed the gentlemen would be ready for a little refreshment. It was outrageous that a visit to a state institution should turn into an interrogation.

Old Äbi's expression had changed; his face had gone pale since his wife had come into the room. Frau Äbi went on speaking, and her voice had nothing whiny about it:

She had had a hard life, she said, and now the only person who had protected her was dead, the only one *him over there* (her calloused hand pointed at Arnold Äbi) had been afraid of. Things had been best when her son had been at home – *one* of her sons, she quickly corrected herself when she saw the sad look in Ludwig's eyes. Yes, her husband had been afraid of Ernst; however drunk he'd been, he'd never dared touch her when Ernst was at home. Of course, he'd been away a lot, but he wrote lots of letters. This letter here, for example. She rummaged round in her old handbag, took out a much-read letter and held it out to Studer. To save her having to get up, Studer went over to her – but he wasn't quick enough. Arnold Äbi leaped forward, his hand outstretched like a claw. The letter! He wanted that letter!

And he would have got it, if it hadn't been for Reinhardt's quick reactions. Just as Äbi's claw was about to fasten onto the letter, Reinhardt stuck out a leg and Äbi fell flat on his face. Calmly, as if nothing had happened, Studer took the letter, unfolded it and asked, "May I read this letter out?" Nods all round. Studer started to read:

Dear Mother,

I have to tell someone. Last night stones were thrown at my window. I was awake, the other students didn't hear. When I looked out, I saw Father waving to me. The college door's locked at night, so I went down to a room on the first floor where there's a window next to some ivy with a thick stem that goes right down to the ground. I clambered down and met Father. He took me to the boiler room. Uncle was on the floor, shot dead. He was in his pyjamas and a coat he'd pulled on over them. Father sent me up to Uncle's room, to fetch a suit, a shirt, socks and an overcoat. We undressed the body and put on the clothes I'd brought. Then Father ordered me to help him carry the body to the graveyard. We put it on Anna's grave. The police were to think Uncle had shot himself out of disappointed love. Then we went back to the boiler room. There was just enough fire to burn the coat, but not the pyjamas; the jacket was wet and soaked in blood. Father made me swear I'd burn the jacket at the first opportunity. I took it, climbed back up the ivy and hid it in my locker, thinking I'd dump it in the central heating furnace the next day. After the post had been distributed, I saw that Herr Wottli had thrown away some wrapping paper. I picked it up and wrapped the pyjama jacket in it. I intended to get up during the night and burn the lot in the central heating furnace but didn't manage to do it. At half past three in the morning Father set off back to Bern on his motorbike. As I was watching him leave, someone suddenly appeared next to me. It was Ludwig. Since I'd once helped him, he promised not to say anything about what he'd seen.

I had to tell you all this, Mother, otherwise I just couldn't bear it. But don't tell anyone I told you, especially not Father.

Lots of love, Mother,

Your son Ernst.

PS Don't tell anyone!

"You're claiming that letter's genuine? Hahaha." Old Äbi laughed. "I've got the only key to the letterbox."

Studer looked at the old woman. Her clothes were shabby; she was wearing a long dress, and heavy shoes stuck out from under the hem. Like many old women, she was sitting with her arms crossed, an elbow clasped in each hand. She stood up, straightened her bent back – truly, the old woman, whom Studer had seen in her illness, looked dignified. And the answer she gave her husband was not scornful, no, there was contempt in it, but it was a dignified contempt.

Noldi thought she was so stupid, she said, speaking to Studer alone, that he assumed she'd have her letters sent to the apartment. For years she'd had the letters she did not want her husband to know about sent to a friend. There was the address, if the sergeant was interested.

Studer took both the letter and the envelope and handed them to the deputy governor to be put in the files.

"So I was right after all, wasn't I, Sergeant?"

Studer shrugged his shoulders. "It wasn't difficult to work out," he said.

A flood of oaths came from Arnold Äbi, but eventually he ran out of breath, and the old woman said, "I wouldn't have given him away if he hadn't . . . if Ernst hadn't . . ."

Her eyes were dry. She took her handkerchief out of her scuffed handbag and blew her nose.

The silence in the room was so profound, the buzzing of a belated fly could be heard. What now? Studer reminded the deputy governor that it was up to him to make the decision.

"Arrest them," said Herr Ochsenbein, "arrest the pair of them."

Old Äbi just stood there, his lower lip hanging down, a baffled look in his schnapps-sodden eyes. But Hungerlott was quicker to come to a decision. One leap – the crash of splintering glass. The warden had jumped out of the window. They all crowded round the shattered windowpanes. Hungerlott was on the ground below, crawling with great difficulty. The man had obviously broken a leg.

Ernst's mother was standing in the middle of the room, her scarf crossed over her breast and her calloused hands clasped. Softly she said:

"Vengeance is mine, saith the Lord."

Then her fingers unclasped. The old woman took the handbag she had jammed under her arm, searched in it and finally brought out a bundle of letters.

"Ernst brought them to me – after Anna died. 'Look after them, Mother,' he said, 'and don't let them get into the wrong hands. Someone wrote them to Anna, they were her only comfort.' But you can keep them, Herr Studer, if you want."

Studer leafed through the bundle. "My Beloved." – "My most dearly Beloved." – "Beloved, are you ill? I feel so very sad. Does your husband treat you kindly? Once you are well again, you must start divorce proceedings. I've talked to your uncle, and he agrees . . ." The sergeant sat down, the buzzing did not disturb him. He read on. "My mother says she looks forward to seeing you. And then we'll try to help your mother. The poor woman . . ."

"What are you reading there, Studer?" the chief superintendent asked. "Shouldn't they go in the files too?"

The sergeant shook his head. "They have nothing to do with the case. Nothing at all. A purely private matter."

"That's fine, then. At least you've not ended up with egg on your face this time."

"I haven't? That's what you think. I couldn't find out why some wrapping paper showed positive in the Marsh test, and the man who could tell me's gone away."

"A witness," the superintendent asked. "You let a witness leave? What did you think you were doing?"

"The witness won't get anything from the will. Not a thing. Though he didn't want anything, so it doesn't matter."

"You're talking nonsense again. Hungerlott wasn't entirely wrong, you know."

Studer's moustache began to quiver. He turned away. His friend the lawyer was standing behind him.

"Münch," said the sergeant, "when are we going to play billiards again?"

"In a fortnight or so," Münch said, clutching his shoulder, which seemed to be hurting badly.

"That's what you get," said Studer, "when you start playing cops and robbers at fifty-eight . . ."